The Reluctant Messiah

A True Norseman

MARK W WARMAN

First Published in 2025

Contact – X @MarkWarman3369

"Sometimes, you can only find Heaven by slowly backing away from Hell."

Carrie Fisher

PART ONE: THE APPRENTICESHIP

CHAPTER ONE

It was almost the mid-1950s in rural Southeast Queensland, and Jack had a four-mile walk to school. It was late in the summer, but the mornings would have a freshness to them. He had to leave home at 7 a.m. as it would take him about an hour to walk there. School started at 8:45 a.m., but he liked getting there early to play with friends before assembly, as it was a nice break from the farm.

Jack was always barefoot as shoes were a luxury at this time. The only pair he had was kept for special occasions.

He was in grade seven, which was his final year of primary school. He was five feet four inches tall, which was tall for a 12-year-old. He had blond hair, and his eyes were deep blue, just like his mum's, though her hair was dark. He wasn't lanky and carried a bit of muscle, given that he worked on the farm nearly every day.

The worst part of the walk was that there was at least three-quarters of a mile to be saved by a shortcut through the Griggs farm, but he had stopped using this years ago, as farmer Griggs chased him one day after he had taken some avocados from the farm during the shortcut. Even after that, Griggs would sometimes verbally abuse Jack while he was walking on the road. Jack felt dread when he had to walk by the farm. The changes to Jack over the last few years had emboldened him over the last weeks to feel very comfortable taking the shortcut through the farm again.

On this day, farmer Griggs caught him in the morning and yelled out to him, "Get off my farm you god damn little shit". Farmer Griggs was two hundred yards away. He did run towards Jack, but Jack could run faster.

Upon returning home from school at 3 p.m. it was a typical summer afternoon, marked by high humidity and temperatures in the mid-30s Celsius. This was the kind of weather that could bring thunderstorms, and the cicadas were deafening in song.

Jack had decided that he was going to retake the shortcut and that it was time to set things straight with Farmer Griggs.

He jumped over the fence and followed the usual track on the farm through where the avocado trees were. Ahead of him, he saw a tractor parked on the side and instinctively knew that farmer Griggs was about. He could feel what was coming as he approached the tractor and readied himself.

Farmer Griggs was probably a few inches taller than Jack but was a lot more solid, as he played football for the local team. As Jack passed the tractor, farmer Griggs ran at him to tackle him to the ground. Jack felt a surge and held his ground while turning around to face Griggs. Griggs lowered himself to tackle Jack around the waist. Using the momentum of him grabbing Jack, he grabbed Griggs under his shoulder pits, twisting him around, then threw him back into the tractor that was six feet behind him. Griggs hit the side of the tractor motor and then fell onto the ground face-first.

Jack was immediately onto him. Griggs was wearing overalls, where Jack grabbed a handful of the overalls at his waist, as well as near the tops of his shoulders. He then picked up Griggs like someone would pick up a small stick and threw him again. Griggs's trajectory had him upside down and going in an upward direction.

He hit the middle of a 12-foot-high avocado tree, upside down, with his head nearly six feet above the ground. At this point, gravity took over, and Griggs fell back to the ground, snapping branches of the tree and landing on the ground with a thud on his back. This was followed by lots of ripe avocados, several of which landed on Griggs. Jack casually walked over to him and could see that Griggs was in a complete state of shock.

He was groaning in pain, but didn't appear to be overly injured. Jack took off his school bag and placed several of the ripe avocados that were around Griggs into his bag. He then stood over him, and as Griggs was looking at him, Jack said in a calm but firm tone, "I'll be walking through your property from now on, and I won't take any more of these. But if ever you need a hand with anything, just ask. Agreed?" Griggs could but nod as he didn't feel like being thrown up into the tree again.

With this, Jack turned away and started walking toward home. After he'd got over the fence and was back onto the normal road, he felt an enormous sense of awe. He'd just been able to repeat something that he'd learned from being around his father.

CHAPTER TWO

Jack Armstrong was born in 1943. His mum and dad had met as high school sweethearts and married early. World War Two had broken out in 1939, and his father was conscripted to join the army in the Australian Imperial Force in the early 1940s.

His mum and dad moved to a suburb of Brisbane to a place called Chermside, where he was to do his training. His father was transferred to a battalion in the same area, and there they continued to train with his father being an infantry soldier. But at the back of their minds, they knew a deployment to war was coming.

In late 1941, the battalion was given orders to prepare to deploy to Singapore. Preparations were made, and they were to leave in February. As fate would have it, the Japanese invaded Singapore in February of 1942, and the battalion was instead sent to Papua New Guinea in late 1942.

At this point, Jack's mum was pregnant with him, and it was a very tearful farewell to her husband as he left. She would not see him for another three years, as he spent this time fighting in the Southwest Pacific against the Japanese till the war was over.

His mother gave birth early the following year and went to live with relatives in a city not far from where they had been staying. It was here that Jack was raised with his mother, her sister, and her family. His father wrote continually to his mother, but never actually spoke about what was going on or where he was, as they were under strict instruction not to communicate their movements.

Like most children, Jack has no memory of this period of his life. The only thing that his mother would remark on later was how he was never sick, never had a scratch on him, and didn't even seem to be bitten by any insects. Other than this, there was nothing remarkable about his early childhood.

Only many years later, Jack could conceptualise what it must have been like for his father to return from war to an over two-year-old child who did not know him. An early memory of his father was that he was hated by him.

Like many returning soldiers, his father was given a forty-hectare block of land in rural southeast Queensland, where they moved in 1946. This was all there was, forty hectares of forest. The block was located on a decent road, which also led to many other blocks that were allocated to other returning servicemen.

His mother and father were lucky in that they had many of their family members living in the area who helped them clear a space and build a modest home. To make a living, Jack's father knew that this land would have to be turned into a farm.

In the meantime, he worked at a sawmill in the local town nearby that had been settled by white people over 100 years before his father's birth. This turned out to be a blessing in that a lot of the property was going to have to be cleared. This meant that his father could both work at the sawmill then cut down trees on his property, and take them into town by horse and cart to sell them to the very sawmill that he worked at.

His mother worked at creating a garden around the home, including vegetables and fruit, as well as having chickens to help feed the family. At the age of five, Jack started school at the one that was four miles away. This was a small school with grades one to seven all in one class with one teacher, with a total of twenty kids.

His mother took him there by horse and picked him up until he was seven years old, when he had to start walking there by himself. His mum was not only pregnant but was also working on the farm more.

It was around this age that Jack started to have memories of not only going to school but also life on the farm. His father was slowly clearing more land and had decided to grow pineapples.

On his return from the war, his father was a platoon sergeant and very much behaved like one towards Jack.

Jack's brother was born when he was seven years old, and as his mum became busy looking after his brother, his father became busy putting Jack to work on the farm. They now had several milking cows, and it was Jack's job to milk them before going to school. This would mean him getting up at 5:30 a.m. with a kerosene lantern as it was still dark, to go and milk the cows by hand and bring the milk back to the house. He would then have breakfast before the hour-long walk to school. Upon returning home from school around 4:00 p.m., his father would always have chores for him, which sometimes included riding the horse to find the cows, often returning after dark.

It was during this period of Jack's life that he started to realise there was something about him that was different from others. He never got tired, never got sick, and never got injured. His mum was aware of this, and his father hated him for it. His father wanted to see him suffer, but Jack never complained or showed signs of weakness. But he would learn that he would have to show these things at times.

Jack, like most children, only wanted to please his father, but didn't always seem to know exactly what his father wanted. His father would perceive this as insolence, and Jack would receive a flogging with his father's belt. Many of his friends would receive the same treatment from their fathers, but for Jack, while he felt the belt hitting him, he felt no pain. He wouldn't even writhe in pain, which only made his father go wilder. What Jack was coming to learn was that he had to show that he was feeling pain, otherwise his father seemed to keep going till he had exhausted himself.

It was also around this time that he was coming to notice that sometimes his mother would have a black eye or bruising to her face when Jack would have breakfast. On asking his mother why, she would just say that she'd run into something.

Around the age of ten, Jack had a very vivid dream of looking at objects like spoons or a saltshaker that were out of reach and having them come into his hand. The dream sat with him for days in his mind. Then one afternoon after school, Jack had the luxury of time to himself. This would happen when his father was in town, running an errand and hadn't left a list of things for him to do. When this happened, he would often go for walks around the property, through the bush, and the paddocks.

Sometimes, when it was hot, there was a particular big eucalyptus tree that he would love to just sit under, as it provided shade and had a nice outlook across a pineapple paddock. Eucalyptus trees drop lots of sticks, leaves, and bark around them, and he would often pick up a stick and just play with it in the dirt while daydreaming.

However, on this day, it was a few days after the dream, and he decided that he would see if he could make a stick come to him. He reached out his hand to a stick that was about three feet away from his hand and imagined it coming to him. Much to his surprise, it did exactly that, and he caught it with his hand. He was actually in shock as he didn't expect it to work. He put down this stick and looked at another one that was a similar distance away, and the same thing happened as with the first stick. This went on with multiple sticks, and Jack slowly piled them up next to him. He was even starting to get sticks to come to him that were twelve to fifteen feet away. As he became more comfortable with what was becoming an experiment, he started to see whether the stick would come without him holding his hand up, but land on the pile that he had created.

Again, to his surprise, he only had to look at the stick and think this, and the stick would come at whatever speed he wanted it to, and it would be on the pile. He then focused on a large branch that was about twelve feet away from him and wondered whether he could make that branch go up in the sky. The branch started going up, and he made it stop with his mind, with the branch being fifteen feet up in the air. He decided to make this branch spin around on its middle axis, which it did. He then made it go faster, and after a while, it was spinning as fast as a bike wheel going down a hill with a whistling noise from the tips of the branch. He decided to leave it like this, and it just kept doing what he had told it to, while he just sat and watched it for several minutes. Then he had the thought that he would make this branch go flying from where it was into the bush that was a couple of hundred feet away. It moved at the speed that he had wanted it to. He heard it crash into the tree line of the bush, given that the branch was spinning so fast and weighed over twenty pounds.

After nearly thirty minutes of playing around with the area, there was a pile of leaves to his left and a pile of sticks to his right, plus a pile of bark, and in front of him, there was a 30-foot square radius of clear ground. He did think about leaving it like this, but he knew that his father would have heaps of questions as to why he had done it and had wasted his time doing this and not some other job. With that, he closed his eyes and imagined the ground being just as it was when he sat down in the first place. He heard what sounded like the rustling of wind through the tops of a tree. He even felt a small gust of wind on his face and opened his eyes to see things pretty much as they were when he sat down about half an hour before. He thought about showing other people this, but an instinct inside him told him to keep it to himself.

The vivid dreams continued to happen with different scenarios, and he found himself experimenting more. One day, he was in the shed where there were bags of feed grain.

He picked up a bag with a hand on each end, as he normally did, which weighed about 20 pounds each. He then decided to pick up four bags stacked on top of each other, which he had never done before, followed by six bags with no effort. He then raised these above his head, and with that, they all managed to topple over him as well as behind him.

To this, Jack laughed as he wasn't focusing on what exactly he wanted to do with the bags of feed, other than pick them up. But this gave him another opportunity. He stood back, looking at the bags of feed on the ground and imagining them all stacked back neatly where they had come from. And just like that, all the bags came off the ground and went back and were neatly stacked without him having to touch them.

It was these experiences that made him feel bolder to experiment more with what was happening. One day, when he was with his father, he was asked to get four bags of feed grain. Where he'd normally grab one bag at a time, on this day, he decided that he'd try and balance four on top of each other to show off to his father.

This worked fine for part of the way getting to the barn where the cows were, but Jack still seemed to be a novice at this supernatural power "thing" or whatever it was, and as he approached the cow shed and with his father watching him, he stumbled with three of the bags falling off, with the top bag splitting and spilling.

He knew straight away that he'd given his father an excuse to give him a flogging, but on this day, his father did something that took him by surprise. His father was a solid man with brown hair and was six feet tall. He moved quickly towards him and said, "You fucking stupid little cunt". Jack had never heard the word "cunt" before, but it must have meant something that you said in anger, as his father raised his right hand and struck him very hard across his face, something he'd never done before.

But here, another strange thing happened. Jack's father had put all his might into the strike on his face, but Jack's head probably only moved an inch, with him feeling no pain. His father pulled his hand back in great pain. For the next couple of weeks, his father protected that hand, and Jack never got another flogging again.

Whatever had happened had given his father quite a fright.

Jack had often heard his father say the word "fuck" in the context of something going wrong in what he was doing, but he never actually swore at him like that till he hit him across his face. Jack did get educated that the words his father spoke were not words to be used lightly.

One day at school, when a bully grabbed Jack by the shirt with the intent to push him over, he pushed the bully's hands away from him and shoved the bully in the chest, with him landing on his back. He said, "You won't be doing that again you fucking cunt?"

The teacher heard him and immediately called out to him and in a loud voice said, "Jack Armstrong, to my office where you're going to get the cane". The cane was a three-foot-long, thin piece of bamboo that was the corporal punishment at the time, though very rarely used by his teacher.

Jack was wearing shorts and was told to bend over on the teacher's desk, while the teacher metered out twenty strikes with the cane to his backside with all the anger he could muster. Of course, none of these were hurting, but he had learnt at this point that he needed to show that it was.

He wasn't sure if he was the greatest actor in the world, but he'd seen enough people writhe in pain to make it look like it hurt. He was overall a very studious student who never played up, so the teacher was quite perplexed that he'd said what he said. After the caning, the teacher told him to sit down and sat down opposite him with beads of sweat on his brow from giving the twenty strikes.

He then asked Jack, "What on Earth made you say that?" He explained that his father used it and that it just came out. The teacher seemed to have some sympathy and explained to Jack very firmly that they were simply words never to be used again, and let him go.

CHAPTER THREE

Jack continued with life on the farm, and the routine now included experimenting with his powers. But he would never cease to be surprised by new powers he would learn, sometimes in circumstances he'd much rather not be in. On another one of his free afternoons, he decided to walk through the bush. There were logs from fallen trees, of which many were over one to two feet wide.

He would sometimes straddle these logs and pick them up, knowing that they weighed over a couple of hundred pounds.

One thing that he didn't think about in doing this was disturbing an ant's nest or something else. This day, he lifted a log and saw a few feet before him a curled-up brown snake that he knew to be a Coastal Taipan.

These are the second most deadly snakes in Australia, and not only was this one over six feet long, but it was also now not very happy. Not only had Jack disturbed it, but the snake felt threatened and coiled, ready to strike. He dropped the log with the intent to flee, but the snake struck him at least twice in the leg. Jack instinctively grabbed it even though he had no idea how to handle a snake.

The snake wrapped around his arm and bit his lower arm several times, until Jack flung it hard, with the snake flying off into the air and into nearby trees. For the first time that he could ever remember, he panicked. He had been firmly warned about these snakes by both his mother and father, and now he'd been bitten by one. This was at a time when there was no real knowledge about immobilising a limb, though there would have been no point, as he had nothing to immobilise it with.

He was at least a fifteen-minute walk out of the bush, with another thirty minutes or so to get back to the house. He ran at first, waiting for the venom to hit him, not knowing what was going to happen. He kept running, as he wanted to get out of the bush to a paddock so that if he collapsed, there was at least some chance that his parents might find him. When he got out onto a paddock, he started to feel pins and needles in his hands and a funny cramping feeling that was happening through both his hands and arms.

Even around his mouth was going numb. He realised that the venom was affecting him and that death was upon him. He started to feel dizzy, plus short of breath for the first time in his life, and sat down on a tree stump. There was a puddle of water in front of him, so he splashed his face. It was at this moment that he decided to look at the snake bite wounds. He checked his legs and could not find anything. He'd felt the snake hit him with its mouth open, biting him. He even saw it bite with its fangs penetrating his skin. He looked at his arm and couldn't see any puncture marks. Strangely, all the symptoms in his hands and mouth started to ease, as did his breathing. As Jack started to feel better, he got up and started walking back home. He never mentioned a word of this to his mother or father, but many years later, he'd discover that what he had experienced was fear for the first time and that he had unwittingly allowed himself to experience the symptoms of hyperventilation. Having survived the snake attack, Jack was starting to feel more invincible. Just how invincible still was not known.

His father would sometimes drink on a Saturday evening. He was not a very pleasant drunk, with arrogance and disdain for the family. On this night, his mother said something to his father that for some reason enraged him. His father had been drinking beer that he'd bought that afternoon and had started drinking port (a fortified wine). His father and mother started arguing in a way that he had not seen before. His father got up and struck his mother across the face, sending her to the ground. This was happening in the kitchen at the far end of the table, as his father pounced on top of his mother and continued to hit her. Jack was screaming at his father to stop, who was oblivious, as his younger brother also started crying. Jack knew that he had to stop his father. In between the kitchen and the dining room was a double-barrel shotgun that was loaded and used to shoot crows that would eat the pineapples. He picked the gun up, and pulled back the hammer. He stood at the other end of the table, pointing it at his father. Jack had used the gun before, as his father had taught him how to use it, but he also knew that the gun contained buckshot cartridges. He could hit both his mum and his father. He again yelled at his father to stop, but his father hit his mother again, oblivious to Jack.

There was a kitchen window just to the left of them that was a pull-up window with eight windowpanes. Jack pointed the shotgun at the window and fired.

There was the loud bang of the gun going off, followed by the shattering of at least four panes of the window, including the splintering of the timber that held them in place. His father immediately stood up and turned around, looking. Jack had the shotgun pointed straight at his father's head. Now that Jack had his father's attention, he said in a firm tone, "Leave her alone".

His father was initially in shock, but something about him took control of the situation, not to mention that he was still very intoxicated. He slowly walked towards Jack, stating, "Give me the gun boy". He continued towards Jack with his hand out, indicating that he wanted the gun. Jack remained steadfast, pointing the gun at his father's head, but he knew that he was not going to be able to pull the trigger on his father.

His father somehow sensed this and grabbed the gun by the barrel, ripping it out of Jack's hands. He then turned the gun on Jack, pointing the barrel right at his head, not less than six inches away.

Jack was slightly numb and didn't know what to do. His mother was screaming. His father looked at him with glazed eyes and pulled the trigger.

CHAPTER FOUR

The hammer on the second barrel clicked, but nothing happened. The gun had misfired. Jack couldn't believe what his father had just done, and grabbed the gun from his father with his left hand on the barrel, and grabbed the gun with the other hand on the butt, with the gun still facing him. He then slammed the end of the butt into his father's face so hard that it broke both his nose and two of his front teeth. He threw the gun to the side and grabbed his father with his left hand by his shirt and with his right hand on his father's belt buckle. He spun him nearly 270 degrees around and threw his father in a horizontal position about six feet across the kitchen into a wall. His father hit it with so much force that the tongue-and-groove timber wall broke in several places. His father dropped to the floor and was clearly in pain, not only from the broken nose but from what would turn out to be several broken ribs from hitting the wall. His mother immediately ran to his father, yelling at Jack to stop.

He had an anger towards his father that he'd never felt. He went over and picked up the shotgun, recocked the hammer, and walked back over towards his father, pointing the gun at him. His mother screamed at him not to shoot. Not only was the cartridge in the gun a dud, but he also didn't feel like shooting his father anyhow. His father was looking at him, and from where they were positioned, they could see into the lounge room. Jack had a curiosity about the dud cartridge, as they rarely misfired. With this, he said to his father, "You see that radio that you play all the fucking time? Well, this is what I think about your radio".

He pointed the gun at the radio, pulled the trigger, and the cartridge fired. He hit the radio, causing it to go flying off the table and then smash into the wall in multiple pieces. Jack stood there in front of his father and unlocked the break action on the shotgun to where you load the cartridges. He pulled out the two empty cartridges, one at a time, and threw them at his father, but not with any real force. He went across to the kitchen where the live cartridges were in a box, grabbed two shells, and returned to standing above his father with the break action still open. With his father watching in fear, he loaded the two shells into the barrel, closed the break action, and then turned and placed the gun back exactly where it was before the start of the whole episode.

He knew he wasn't going to be able to sleep in the house that night, so he grabbed a kerosene lantern and went off to the barn and slept on the bales of hay. He didn't return the following day. Jack knew that he would be sharing the barn with a snake that Jack called "Hank the carpet snake". He knew that Hank was harmless and not venomous, but it was three times as thick as the brown snake and had a habit of moving around the shed that could be unnerving, as sometimes you would walk in, look up, and Hank would be directly above you. Jack's father liked the carpet snakes being in the shed because they fed on the rats and mice, as they were a type of Python. The following day, Jack knew that his mum would be busy with his father, so he went and got one of the horses, just putting a bridle on it, rode it bareback and went up to a dam. Here, he had great fun taking the horse into the water and jumping off it into the dam, as well as riding it in the shallower water, something that Jack's father would never have let him do.

He returned to the house on Monday morning to find his mother fixing breakfast. She turned to him, and he was shocked at the amount of bruising that she had on her face. His mother burst into tears and came to him, wrapping her arms around him and rubbing his back, and she said quietly into his ear, "I love you very much, I was worried you'd gone". After a while, they broke the hug, and she asked if he wanted breakfast.

His mum brought him over breakfast that consisted of porridge topped with butter, milk, and a drizzle of honey that came from the farm. There was also a boiled egg in a special cup that you cracked the top off, and stuck fingers of bread called soldiers into the soft yolk. While she was putting the bread in front of him, he asked about his father and said, "How is he?" She replied that she was concerned about him and that they might have to take him into town to see the doctor. Jack said that he could get the horse and cart ready and put one of their single mattresses on the back for his father to lie on, and his mother agreed.

Jack did say, "How are we going to explain this?" His mother had given this some thought, and the story she had was that his father had come off the horse while in a full gallop. Jack wished that this was exactly what had happened. He then said, "But what about you?" While looking at her bruised face. She again broke into tears, but Jack had a moment where he said something to her that would surprise him again. He said, "Kneel in front of me mum, and let me touch your face". His mum did this, and Jack gently put his hands on his mum's face and visualised the bruises going away, and with that, they did. She looked just as beautiful as she always did.

She knew what had happened as the pain had left her face and rushed to the bathroom to look in a mirror that was on the cupboard door above the sink. She came back and said to Jack, "How did you do that?" He genuinely said, "I have no idea". She then said, "Could you do that to your father?" Jack replied rather bluntly, telling his mum that he had no intention to even try that with his father. Not only had he beaten up his mum, but his father had tried to kill him the other night. Jack felt that his father should suffer for that, and his mum wasn't about to argue with him.

Jack organised the horse and cart and mattress, and for the first time since the night, he went in to see his father. His mother had applied bandages to his nose as well as some bandages around his chest. His father was in a semi-conscious state and didn't seem to be very aware that Jack was in the room. Jack stated to his mom that he would carry his father out to the mattress on the cart, where his mum agreed. His father was clearly in a lot of pain as Jack moved him, but Jack picked him up with no effort at all and carried him out, and gently placed him on the mattress in the back of the cart.

The weather was mild, but they placed a sheet over him, as well as propped a straw hat in a comfortable way over his head so that he wouldn't get sunburnt. With his mother, brother, and Jack at the front of the cart, they took the journey into town to find the Doctor. It was a weekday, and the doctor was quite busy, but Jack's mom explained that they had a medical emergency. The doctor came out to see Jack's father, and Jack said that he could bring him into the surgery. The doctor agreed. The doctor redressed his father's nose with plaster so that it was more stable, then removed the bandaging around his father's chest, and applied tape that seemingly made the chest more stable to cause less pain. The doctor explained to his mother that it was only going to be time that would heal the wounds, and that his father was to rest for at least several weeks. He also gave his mother a script for some painkillers, which Jack's mum went and got for his father. Jack carried his father back out to the cart and moved it on to the local grocery store, which was close to the pharmacy where his mum was. He had some medicine of his own in mind.

His mum returned with several bottles of liquid morphine and a couple of boxes with Beck's powder sachets in them. Jack said to his mum, "Can we have an ice cream?" Which was something his father never let them have when they were in town. His mum didn't hesitate and gave him the money to go in and get all three of them an ice cream cone, with a scoop of vanilla ice cream on top. Jack had had this before when he had run errands to town by himself, but it never ceased to surprise him just how nice it was. At least the episode with his father had some upsides. They returned home, and he carried his father back into bed. Fortunately, it was wintertime, and the fields were full of corn, which was a rotational crop used between the pineapple season and needed little attention. Jack spoke to his mum about what chores needed to be done on the farm, and he went about doing these. He hadn't seen his father for about four days as he simply didn't feel like going in to see him. But on this day, his mother told him that his father was more comfortable, particularly with the painkillers on board.

He went in and sat down on his father's side of the bed. Their eyes met, and Jack could tell that his father was feeling remorseful and in shock at what had happened. He told his father about all the chores that he was doing and even asked his father if there was anything that he happened to be missing, as he was more than happy to do those jobs.

His father then did something that he'd never done before. He put out his hand onto Jack's hand, gently holding it, then patting Jack's forearm, said to him, "You're doing a good job". The next few weeks were some of the best in Jack's life. He had the farm to himself, going about chores that he quite enjoyed doing, as well as getting to spend lots of quality time with his mum, who would also help him out with some chores. His father seemed back to his normal self within about a month and was starting to slowly do things around the farm. The big difference was that he treated Jack with respect and never again yelled at him or hit his mum.

Of course, there would be times when he would express frustration if Jack wasn't doing a particular job properly, but that only felt natural. As the year drew to a close, Jack had the opportunity to go on to high school the following year, but he was quite happy on the farm. It was growing to the point that even with his mum and other family members helping, his father would have to employ people to help with the pineapple harvest. Jack's father knew that he was looking at going to high school, and to Jack's surprise, his father offered him ten shillings a week to stay on the farm and work for him.

It was during this period that Jack started to learn that he could read people's minds. This would prove to be a very interesting exercise in that often he was hearing stuff that he simply didn't want to hear, and it would take him many years to work out how to censor it. But fortunately, he learnt how to turn it on and off and even to categorise what it was that he wanted to hear. He also would come to realise that there was what people were thinking, as well as their memories that he could also retrieve.

With regard concerning his father, this worked well in that he often knew straight away if his father needed something. One day, he read his father's thoughts that he needed a shovel. Jack said straight away to his father that he would go back to the barn and get it, and ran, returning less than ten minutes later.

Despite not going to high school, he had an insatiable desire to learn and read about the world. He would do this by going into the local town library, borrowing books and reading them in the evening. The librarian got to know him quite well as he would often start asking for books that she didn't have in stock. But she could sometimes order them from other libraries for him. Jack found that not only could he understand all the information that he read, but that he was able to conceptualise it, and even have good critical thinking skills around all the information.

It was also during this time that Jack learnt that he could connect with animals, to the point that they would be tame around him. This even included him having an adventure into the bush one day, where he went looking for the Coastal Taipan that had bitten him. He was finding that he had instincts about where animals and even people were in proximity, even if he couldn't see them. He came out into an area of bush and knew that the snake was just in front of him, curled up near a log.

He sat on the ground a few feet in front of the snake. At first, the snake didn't move, but eventually, it lifted its head and looked at him. Jack even enticed it to come to him, saying in his mind to the snake that it was very safe to be in his presence. The snake moved towards him, gently sliding over his crossed legs, then moving around to his back. It slid up over his back and shoulder before moving away and curling up again, enjoying the sun. Without saying it out loud, he thanked the snake and apologised for disturbing it.

The cows would also no longer wander off, as Jack had a gentle talk to them about how inconvenient it was when he had to go and find them. He was rather amused that the cows would now always be easy to find and would never wander off the property again. The greatest delight that he had was with the horses that they still had on the farm, despite now having a tractor. His father had wanted to sell them, but Jack had said that he would take care of them, with his father agreeing. With regards to the horses, he simply enjoyed riding them. He found that not only could he communicate with them, but they did not tire when he was riding them. He even found that he could make the horse go into a trot, a canter or even a gallop without having to instruct the horse physically to do it. The horse would even slow up, stop, and turn without him having to pull on the reins. Jack even got bold, if not lazy, to not put on the reins and saddle, and would often ride the horse bareback while holding their mane, which was great fun.

There was a harmony on the farm that could only be described as peaceful. The farm had good crops and was very prosperous. After ten years, during which Jack worked from the age of twelve, he had saved close to £1000. His father had given him raises without him having to ask, as his father saw his son as a very reliable and hard worker. In the early 1960s, he was getting nearly £3 a week. Jack didn't mind this at all as he got free board and lodging and didn't spend a lot when he went to town.

But as Jack would come to discover, life changes, and one must adapt and change with it, even if a change is for the worse. For both his mother and father, that nightmare came from the start of the Vietnam War and the introduction of conscription. This came via a letter in 1965 that informed Jack that he was to present himself to a Barracks in Brisbane in three months.

CHAPTER FIVE

The clock was ticking down, and Jack was excited about the coming adventure. The routine before harvest was working on the paddocks with his father, getting things ready to pick the pineapples.

They'd all have breakfast, lunch and dinner together at the house, but morning and afternoon tea were done under the shade of a tree near whichever paddock they were working on.

If it wasn't raining, they'd sit under a nice shady tree, light of fire, and put a billy can on it with tea boiling away. It was coming into the summer, and his mother liked to start making Christmas cakes early, so they would have pieces of this wrapped up in aluminium foil and a cup of tea or two.

Jack would go on to discover that it wasn't the greatest cup of tea, as it was over-boiled and quite bitter. But he always took a small container of honey with him and had at least two teaspoons in the cup so that it wasn't so bitter. His father disapproved of him having sugar in it. But given that his father was the beekeeper on the farm, he didn't mind Jack using honey.

His father never talked about the war, and it was a known thing within the family that it was a taboo subject. But on this particular day, while having morning tea, his father started talking to him about what to expect in going to training camp and into the army.

He told Jack, "They will try and break you down and make you an obedient robot", before going into what it was like for himself in the early part of his training. His father's number one bit of advice was just to listen to what they say, do what they say, and never answer back. Regarding the army, his father told him, "You are gonna meet some pretty hard bastards who will give you a very hard time. There will even be some who will try and pick a fight, but I know that you'll be okay", while smiling. It was never spoken about when Jack's father hit him across the face. For Jack's father, he might as well have just gone and hit his hand as hard as he could against a steel pole. There were some broken bones in his hand that took a while to heal. But he was never going to admit to that.

Jack's father then said, "War is hell, but just keep calm". He went on to explain how one of his bases was bombed, with some dropping all around him. His father said, "Your life is never the same when you see a mate blown to pieces and not knowing if you're next".

He then went on to describe a particular graphic event, where hundreds of Japanese troops came across an open area, and attacked them when they were low on ammunition.

They couldn't gun them down fast enough, and by the time they were near them, they didn't have time to reload their weapons, and it ended up being hand-to-hand combat.

His father then said, "Nothing ever really prepares you for killing a man in such vicious circumstances until you do it". Then Jack's father said something to him that would stay with him for the rest of his life, "When it comes to killing, never hesitate and don't let up until it's done".

Jack had done his fair share of killing sick or impaired animals, plus pests on the farm with a rifle, but he hadn't really given any thought that he was going to be heading off to war with the potential for him to shoot and kill a human being.

At that time, he believed that the war was the right thing and that he would be doing his duty to his country. Then the day came, and they drove to the nearest train station to say goodbye. His mother was crying, and his father looked like he was about to cry. But they were confident that they were going to get to see him before he went overseas. That would be the last time that Jack got to see his mother. Jack left early so he could spend several days in Brisbane. He also went to a barber and got his head clipped to the skull, anticipating the fact that the army was going to do that to him anyhow, based on what his father had told him. He was determined to maintain at least some level of control over his life.

He went to the barracks in Brisbane, where they conducted medicals, measured them up for clothes, and corralled them onto buses for the overnight trip down to the Kapooka Army barracks, which were in New South Wales.

He could see that there was going to be one issue he was going to face. He was now six feet five inches with broad shoulders, and at this stage, he wasn't seeing anyone as tall as him. Jack was starting to learn very quickly about "small man syndrome". The posturing had begun by those around him.

On arriving at Kapooka Army base, the chaos started as soon as they started to disembark the buses. A recruit instructor (RI) got onto the bus and was yelling at them to get off. But no one could do anything right.

The recruit instructor stood in the middle of the aisle of the bus and yelled at one guy, "Get the fuck off my bus". The guy stood up, and the RI yelled at him, "Get the fuck out of my face". The poor guy then sat down, only to be yelled at again for not getting off the bus. On getting off the bus, Jack immediately regretted getting his hair clipped to the bone. An RI screamed at him, "What the fuck are you? A skinhead?"

That was to become Jack's nickname for the duration of the training, even though he had no idea what it meant at the time. He even had to line up with all the other recruits in the queue to get their hair cut. On sitting down in the chair, an RI said to the barber, "Make sure this cockhead looks like he did when he came out of his mama's arse".

Jack could see the barber in the mirror, and he had a smirk. Their eyes met, and Jack also slightly smiled and raised his eyebrows. The barber very quietly said, "This wasn't the brightest idea, was it?" while running the clipper over his head and removing what little there was of about five days of growth.

Jack's father had warned him of all this. He felt like laughing at some of the extremes of the recruit instructors' behaviours. But he knew that he had to keep a straight face and do exactly what they said, knowing that often even that wouldn't always please them.

They would be lined up, bunched up, marched, get abused, had to run everywhere, march again, crawl through mud and pipes, and do obstacle courses, only to have the whole cycle start the next day from 6:00 a.m. to 10:00 p.m. for 8 weeks.

Physically, Jack loved it, given that none of this was taxing to him. Doing push-ups, chin-ups, being screamed at to "get down and give me fifty" when it was of no effort at all.

Even the obstacle courses were great fun, including the running and marching in formation.

He even got to love Australian versions of the US Army Candace's that would happen where the RI would sing the line in tempo to the marching run, and the whole squad would repeat the same line in tempo. They even did the Australian version of "Two Old Ladies".

"Two old ladies were lying in bed."
"One turned over to the other and said."
"I wanna be in Army Australia"
"Live that life of blood and danger."

"Army Australia".
"Blood and danger"

They got put in dorms with bunk beds, and fate would have it that he would share his bunk bed with a guy named Ronnie. Ronnie was two inches taller than Jack, with sun-bleached blonde hair and blue eyes like Jack's, and the first person he had ever met that he had to look up to. Though Ronnie was currently sporting a skinhead just like Jack.

He loved Ronnie's free spirit. Ronnie was brought up on the northern beaches of Sydney with a very wealthy family. He'd gone to a very prestigious private school and was a top swimmer at a highly competitive level. He had gone to high school and on to university to do a law degree, with his father pushing him to become an Olympic swimmer. While Ronnie had not been conscripted, his father had plans to override this with money and connections should it happen.

Ronnie, on the other hand, had no plans to do anything his father wanted and quietly went off and enrolled in the army. He had basically run away from home, sending his parents a letter from Kapooka to tell them where he was. He knew that his father would be furious, with his mother beside herself, and loved the very thought of it.

Ronnie was not as solid as Jack was at the start of boot camp, and the recruit instructors at first called him "stick insect", which later turned into the nickname "stick". He, like most who got into the physical side of boot camp, couldn't avoid getting bigger muscles.

Being a tall person, chin-ups can be harder to do as you have to lift a lot more weight. One day, Jack was with Ronnie, who was struggling to do even five chin-ups. And just like Jack would be with the horses, he channelled a part of himself into Ronnie, and Ronnie proceeded to do fifty chin-ups without effort.

He would later share with Jack that this feeling came over him, with his body feeling like it weighed 20 pounds. Jack replied, "I know". He had found the first person in his life that he was going to share what was going on for him. The RI's noted that they had become good friends, and because of their height and similar looks, would call them "the sin sisters" and "faggots".

Jack had to get Ronnie to explain what this meant, as he had with regard to him being called a "skinhead".

Jack didn't need to sleep at night, and he would just lie on the bunk with his feet hanging over the end of the bed, daydreaming. Ronnie was on the top bunk and would toss and turn. This one night, Jack closed his eyes and imagined speaking to Ronnie.

He said to Ronnie in his mind, "I want you to listen to me and don't reply out loud. Lie on your back, close your eyes and imagine that you're saying, 'I can hear you' back to me". Ronnie did this, and Jack heard him in his mind.

It was as though he was imparting a part of his powers onto Ronnie, and every night at lights out, they would lie, spending some of the eight hours that they were allocated for sleep communicating with each other. Jack shared his life and his stories as Ronnie shared his.

Ronnie could speak fluent French and taught Jack how to do so as well, even though they never said a single word out loud to each other. One day, when they were at the rifle range, they had a moment together out of earshot of the other recruits and the recruit instructors.

They had an out-loud conversation in French about the terrible lunch they had just had, and completely understood each other. Both looked at each other in amazement, and Jack continued in French, "C'est putain de genial" (That was fucking awesome).

Jack then said they should both learn Vietnamese, where they both eagerly agreed.

An area where both Jack and Ronnie excelled was at the rifle range. For the first three weeks of training, they handled their weapons with no ammunition but had to learn how to dismantle them, maintain them and put them back together. They would often sleep with them, and very rarely did they not have the weapon on them. If a cadet happened to leave their rifles somewhere unattended, the whole group would be assembled, and the culprit found.

This would then be followed by the whole group having to do a ten-kilometre run or some other physically arduous tasks. Collective punishment was the means to get the group to pull rogue cadets into line, and they'd receive a beating by the group if they stuffed up when the recruit instructors weren't about. Jack didn't like this, as he felt the weaker were being punished, but it was a primitive form of getting the weak to get their act together or to be stretchered out.

Ronnie had never handled a gun in his life, and Jack showed him and even coached him during some of their evening discussions. When they started on the firing range, Jack had communicated to Ronnie about pointing the weapon at the target and imagining it hitting exactly where you wanted it to. He also said to make the spread uneven within the target so that it didn't look like you were being 100 per cent precise; otherwise, it may draw attention to them. Attention it did, the recruit instructors noticed that both Jack and Ronnie never missed their targets on the shooting range. One RI went as far as to manipulate their weapons to make them inaccurate, yet they still hit their targets.

Jack was coming to the attention of Corporal Oakley. He was five feet four inches and had some serious issues with both Jack and Ronnie, who towered over him. Jack was often subjected to fifty to one hundred push-ups simply because Corporal Oakley could command him to. He could tell that the other recruit instructors didn't particularly like Corporal Oakley, and on this one day, he decided that he'd had enough as well. Jack was walking out of the barracks towards the Mess Hall as Corporal Oakley was approaching. Corporal Oakley picked on Jack's uniform even though there was nothing wrong with it. He was immediately told to get down and do one hundred push-ups. He did these quickly and without effort. Corporal Oakley ordered him to do another hundred.

He could tell Corporal Oakley had some suspicions, as Jack never showed fatigue doing push-ups and did the other hundred without effort. Corporal Oakley again told him to do another hundred, at which point Jack decided to do something different. He lowered himself to the ground with his nose just one inch above the ground and held it there for a second. He then went back up and held himself at the top of the push-up for another second while doing the count. Corporal Oakley immediately knew that Jack was taking the piss. In a rage, he walked over to Jack and kicked him as hard as he could in the stomach as he was in the up position of the push-up. And just like when Jack's father hit him across the face, Corporal Oakley might as well have just gone and kicked a suspended tree log. He immediately fell back, holding his shin in agony.

Jack allowed himself to tumble over but had not felt a thing. Sergeant Barnett, the senior recruit instructor, had observed the whole thing and walked over, telling Jack to stand at attention. Sergeant Barnett ordered Corporal Oakley to get up off the ground and walk over to the Barrack Headquarters.

With Jack standing there at attention with Sergeant Barnett next to him, they both watched Corporal Oakley limp until he got about twenty yards away. At this point, Sergeant Barnett wiped grass off Jack's uniform while saying, "We have fucking standards to keep Skinhead". He then ordered Jack to follow him. They also went to the barracks headquarters to see Captain Blackmore, who was in charge of the platoon. As they were nearing the entrance, there was a bench seat outside, and Sergeant Barnett ordered Jack to sit there until he was called.

It was a standing order that the recruitment instructors were in no way to physically assault the recruits. It happened anyhow and was tolerated, as it was seen at times as a necessary thing to do. Corporal Oakley had crossed the line, and Captain Blackmore and Sergeant Barnett were not at all happy, plus it had given them the perfect opportunity to get rid of him. He had argued that Jack was insubordinate and there was something highly suspicious about just how good he was as a recruit. Corporal Oakley even went as far as to say that Jack was a "commie" spy. Jack sat there in the hot sun before Corporal Oakley walked out and sat down on the bench next to him, as he had been ordered to. Sergeant Barnett was right behind him and told Jack to follow him, and they went inside to Captain Blackmore's office.

Sergeant Barnett sat down on the opposite side of the table with Captain Blackmore and told Jack to take a seat in front of them. Jack was already aware of what was going on, but he knew he would just have to go along with letting them say what they had to say. Captain Blackmore stated that Sergeant Barnett had informed him that Jack was a very promising recruit. Jack was then asked about his background, and he told them about how he had grown up and worked on the family farm until he was twenty-two years of age before he was conscripted.

He then added that his father had served in the Pacific during World War Two. It just so happened that Sergeant

Barnett had also served there, though he had not met Jack's father, but was aware of the battalion.

He said to Jack, "They took on some heavy shit". Sergeant Barnett had been the one who had first called him "skinhead" and had seen that Jack had a bit of fire in him. Sergeant Barnett was very blunt in asking if he was willing to follow orders under all circumstances. Jack yelled, "Yes sir".

Captain Blackmore could see that Corporal Oakley was a complete idiot in seeing Jack as a communist spy. He thought, why would a spy waste their time as a simple "grunt" in an infantry Battalion who would not be fed any more intel than cornflakes and long-life milk? Neither Jack nor Captain Blackmore had any idea that in over two years, he would be giving very valuable information to the Viet Cong.

Captain Blackmore told Jack to keep on doing what he was doing and that he would turn out to be a fine soldier. Jack was told, "If you could tell Corporal Oakley to come back into the office, you're dismissed".

He stood and saluted at attention while yelling, "Yes sir", turned around and left the office. On going outside, he knew that Sergeant Barnett was not watching him.

He stood at attention in front of Corporal Oakley and said in a robotic way, "SIR, Captain Blackmore has instructed me to tell you to get your short arse inside. I also hope your shin is hurting like hell as you are a fucking little cunt", before saluting and walking back to his barracks. Corporal Oakley's face went red with rage, and he jumped up to follow Jack,

41

only to hear Sergeant Barnett yell, "Corporal Oakley, Captain Blackmore's office, NOW".

In Captain Blackmore's office, Corporal Oakley said that Jack had just called him a fucking little cunt. Sergeant Barnett said, "Well you are a fucking little cunt. You're not an RI here anymore. Go pack your bags as you're on the next bus out of here".

Corporal Oakley was sent to a battalion in Sydney that went on to Vietnam. He would return to Australia three years later in a body bag.

CHAPTER SIX

Into the final three weeks of their training, the platoon was much more in sync, and the recruit instructors were yelling a lot less. Here, they began to undergo more basic training as soldiers by going off into the bush and learning skills such as navigation, formation, and army camping. Jack had been made section leader for his group and felt right at home in the bush.

He had done a few years in the Boy Scouts at school, and his skills in navigation and camping did not go unnoticed by Sergeant Barnett. Even on very simple tactical exercises, Jack's ability to locate people was very good at finding "the enemy" as they played basic war games of hide and seek.

The graduation from recruit training was coming close, and they were asked to fill out forms expressing where they may wish to go and what skills they had to offer. Jack had made a point of reading Sergeant Barnett's mind about how the process of assignment to Battalions was going to happen. Captain Blackmore would receive a list of Battalions that needed recruits, and he and the recruit instructors would sit down and discuss who to allocate where. One night, while lying in bed, Jack was able to see the list and even knew where these battalions were. He also wanted Ronnie and himself to stay together, and there seemed to be the perfect opening for them that would be not only an exciting opportunity, but it would be on Ronnie's turf. During the meeting where they allocated the recruits, Jack had planted the idea of where he and Ronnie should go in Sergeant Barnett's mind. The Sergeant advocated that both Jack and Ronnie were by far the top recruits and that they shouldn't simply be sent off to the "meat grinder" of infantry battalions. He argued that they had far more to offer the army and that they should be sent on an assignment that would enhance their skills and, by proxy, that of the army's.

With this, Jack and Ronnie were assigned to the 1st Topographical Survey Troop at Randwick Barracks in Sydney to learn the skills of map-making and reconnaissance. Ronnie was particularly excited as he wanted to show Jack Sydney.

The day came for the marching out, where, in full dress uniform, they went out onto the parade ground, marching to where the whole battalion of recruits formed. Jack's family were not able to make it, but Ronnie's father and mother were there.

He got to meet them after the parade and immediately took a dislike to Ronnie's father, who had a pompous arrogance and a complete disdain for what his son was doing. Ronnie, however, appeared to have no feelings regarding this and felt very proud of what he had achieved over the last two months.

They turned up at Randwick Barracks in late 1965 as newly minted privates in the Australian Army. What struck them both straight away was how much more relaxed it was than the intense two months they had experienced at recruit training. They were also happy that the men they were working with were all very well-educated, smart people, and there were no schoolyard bullies.

They were at first outsiders, and they were still the tallest in the group, but their colleagues would come to see that they were both very capable, intelligent men themselves.

It was coming up towards Christmas, and they were going to have the luxury of two weeks off. While Jack had nearly a thousand pounds in his bank account, Ronnie had four times as much. Jack laughed when Ronnie told him, but he also knew how Ronnie had earned it.

Ronnie's father had not given him much pocket money as he went through high school, nor as he went through university, though his father also looked down on the idea of Ronnie working a part-time job.

This placed Ronnie in a difficult position as a lot of his friends had heaps of money to spend. Ronnie had seen that his friends liked to use marijuana and even cocaine, and made a job for himself of getting it and selling it to them for a neat profit.

On coming to Sydney, Jack could see that he'd had a rather sheltered life. He was quite content on the farm, and had it not been for conscription, he might have just stayed there.

He had devoured many books in the library, reading about other countries, political systems and religions, but he never really read any of the fiction books. There was a whole world that Jack was not aware of, and it was only through meeting Ronnie that he started to see that there was much more to the world.

They had spent two months in dorm rooms at Kapooka, sharing a bunk bed and were now sharing a room with two single beds at Randwick Barracks. Ronnie suggested that during those two weeks off, they go get themselves a room each at the Chevron Hilton Hotel near Kings Cross. Ronnie shouted Jack, and little did Jack know that the room he got, which had a great view of the Sydney Harbour Bridge, cost more than 3 months of his wages.

Ronnie explained that the hotel was very posh and that they were going to have to be well-dressed. Jack only had a handful of casual clothes on him, and the rest was all military uniform. Instead of going out and buying new clothes, Jack suggested to Ronnie that they wear their formal dress uniforms around the hotel and in town. It wasn't until they came to go out for a night on the town in Kings Cross that this became a problem with a Navy base nearby. Ronnie did say that one problem with this was that they'd only been issued with a single-dress uniform. But Ronnie was a man who could get things and procured them each two extra sets of full-dress uniforms.

It would turn out to be two weeks of sheer wonder for Jack, staying in one of the most beautiful cities in the world, while staying in the most luxurious hotel in Australia. They would meet up for breakfast downstairs in the hotel and have eggs Benedict with coffee. Jack knew his mum would have loved this dish. They spent a day walking across to the New South Wales Art Gallery that was built in the late 1800s, through the Botanic Gardens and on to Circular Quay.

While Jack had been to Brisbane on many occasions, Sydney was a whole new level of beauty and wonder. Ronnie was thoroughly enjoying being the tour guide. He was even testing Jack with meals and foods that Jack had never had before. One night, they sat down and had a dozen Sydney Rock oysters each with freshly squeezed lemon juice on them, followed by a steak tartare and Beef Wellington. These foods were from an alien world to Jack, but he loved them.

Ronnie had promised his mom that he would be home for Christmas. His parents had a beachfront home in the suburb of Manly that required a ferry ride on Sydney Harbour from Circular Quay. They both turned up in full-dress uniforms. This was, in part, an unpleasant day with Ronnie's father becoming intoxicated and belittling them. They did, however, have a glorious lunch and afterwards, Jack was standing out on the balcony admiring the view of the Pacific Ocean.

Ronnie's father came out to him with a glass of whiskey in hand and started to rib Jack about coming from a farm. Jack turned to him, and looking him directly in the eye, calmly said, "Sir, I want to try dangling you off this balcony using one hand around your ankle. You up for it you arrogant piece of shit?" Ronnie's father's face went pale as he could tell Jack would do just that, and Ronnie's father immediately left, leaving Jack to enjoy the view. Ronnie was apologetic after they left, but Jack reassured him that it had been a great day and that he'd loved seeing the area and his parents' house. Jack told him what he had said to his father, and he became Ronnie's hero, as he would never have dared to say that to his dad.

The biggest adventure was yet to come. It was a Friday night, and Ronnie was taking Jack up to Kings Cross. This was Sydney's Red-Light District, full of bars, strip clubs, brothels and even takeaway food places where Jack got to experience the delight of a doner kebab. On a Friday night, it was bustling with people, and Jack loved it. He had tried beer a few times in his life, but he'd never felt any effect from it. Ronnie took him into a strip bar, and Ronnie was buying rounds of stubbies of Victorian Crown lager.

It was a surreal experience to be watching women coming out and stripping themselves naked. While Jack could appreciate beauty, he had never had a sexual desire in his life. He had never had an erection or masturbated, had never had a girlfriend, or had sex. His local library didn't have any books

48

on this, and while he had an idea about procreation from watching a bull hump a cow or the dogs having sex, he'd not given it any thought beyond that animals had sex to make babies. These women were indeed beautiful, but at this time, Jack simply didn't get why all these men watching were getting excited and carrying on.

At this point, he had consumed eight stubbies of beer and did not feel a thing. Ronnie, on the other hand, was becoming very jovial, and Jack knew that he was becoming intoxicated. Ronnie slapped his hand on Jack's shoulder and told him that he should let go and go with it. Jack laughed at this and then in his mind, decided to feel the effects of the alcohol in his body.

Suddenly, the effect of eight beers hit him, and the room was spinning. For the first time in Jack's life, he felt nausea in his stomach and had a feeling that he was going to throw up. He became lost in this and could feel that he was losing control when Ronnie again grabbed him by the shoulder and said to him, "Are you okay?" This immediately pulled Jack out of what he was feeling, and he was back to normal again. Ronnie laughed and said, "Maybe we should take this a bit more slowly next time".

Jack and Ronnie were sitting near the bar, wearing their full-dress uniforms, when they were approached by three men who were from the Navy. They were immediately antagonistic, and Jack knew straight away that they wanted to fight. Jack didn't want anything to do with it, but could tell that Ronnie wanted to rumble. For Jack, this was going to be all for entertainment, just like watching the women strip themselves naked. Ronnie was antagonistic back, and one of the Navy guys threw a punch at him. What surprised Jack though, was Ronnie's moves. He blocked the punch and did a high kick, knocking the Navy man to the ground unconscious. Two of his friends rushed Ronnie, and again, Ronnie used moves, dispatching the other two gentlemen to the ground within seconds. Two bouncers immediately came and went straight for Ronnie, where they ended up being relieved of their jobs for the night in short order. With five men lying on the ground moaning in pain, Ronnie said to Jack with a smile, "I think we'll leave now".

On getting outside, Jack said to Ronnie, "What were those moves?" He replied, "Kung Fu". Jack had read about this before, but had never seen it, nor did he know that his friend was quite proficient in it. He immediately said to Ronnie, "I wanna know more about this".

The big difference between Ronnie and Jack was that Jack was born with powers even he still didn't understand. Ronnie, on the other hand, had been born and lived a life totally different to Jack's. This was a life of emotional highs and lows, pain and suffering. Ronnie also enjoyed sex, getting high, getting drunk and even brawling with a free spirit of getting a kick out of it all. Jack had experienced none of this. Ronnie had said to Jack that he was going to get a woman to take back to his room to have sex all night long. The sex show that they'd watched had Ronnie worked up, and he needed to let off some steam. There were prostitutes in the street, and

Ronnie approached one. A negotiation happened, and with that, Ronnie was gone, leaving Jack by himself in Kings Cross.

He knew where the hotel was, so it wasn't as though he was lost, but he certainly was in an environment that was completely unfamiliar to him. He didn't feel like going back to the hotel at that time and wandered around the areas of King's Cross, just people-watching. He would be approached by prostitutes offering their services as well as people offering him drugs to buy. For the first time in his life, he also saw people begging. Naively, he pulled out a wad of £1 notes and gave one to a beggar.

This came to the attention of a man who had been watching him as he wandered around and started going down side streets, exploring this majestic place. The man who had seen him go down a dark street followed him, and when he saw the opportune time, said to Jack, "Give me your money". Jack turned around, and the man had a knife pointing directly at him. He didn't say anything at first, and the man became more agitated, repeating, "Give me your fucking money". Jack simply replied to him, "It's my money, not yours". It was clear to him that the man was under the influence of drugs and that Jack's life was of low priority over the money that he had in his pocket.

He grabbed the man's hand that was holding the knife with a firm grip, and with his other hand, grabbed the man under his neck with his fingers firmly at the bottom of his jaw and threw him up against the nearest wall. He put upward pressure on the man whose feet left the ground while proceeding to crush the man's hand that was holding the knife. The man dropped the knife after his hand was broken, and Jack let him fall back onto his feet, where he fell to the ground. Jack turned and just walked away.

Strangely, he didn't feel anything about the whole episode, but decided it was time to walk back to the hotel. He came back onto the main street and was walking along past women soliciting themselves, and then he saw her. She had a natural beauty that took Jack by surprise. He liked that she was reasonably tall at five feet eight inches.

She didn't need make-up to be beautiful, even though her face was covered in it. She said to him, "Are you up for some fun honey?" Jack stopped and spoke to her. He had a sense about her and that there was more to her than other people that he'd met that night.

He asked her how much it was for her service, and she replied, "£5 for the night". He found himself saying yes and said that he had a room at the Hilton Hotel, which immediately impressed her. He had read her mind and knew her name was Nancy, although she was working by another name.

They talked on the way back to the hotel, and it turned out that Nancy had grown up on a farm in rural New South Wales. She was three years younger than him and, at nineteen years of age, was far more streetwise than him.

The dress she was wearing was very tight-fitting and showed her voluptuous hourglass figure, with her large breasts nearly falling out of the top. Jack knew at the hotel that she could be refused entry as she didn't meet the dress standard, and it was clear that she was a prostitute. What he didn't realise was that the hotel staff were familiar with patrons coming back from Kings Cross with sex workers, and some even got a commission from the prostitutes for allowing them into the hotel.

For Jack, he simply wanted Nancy's company. When they got to the room, he gave her £10 instead and said that he simply wanted to be in her company. This made her more relaxed, and she suggested that they lie down on the bed and cuddle while they talked. They did this for a short while, and Jack just found himself enjoying her company and the conversation.

Nancy said that she was feeling cold and that they should get naked together and get under the bedding. She did this by not implying that they were going to have sex, but simply to get naked and cuddle.

Ironically, Jack wanted to get out of his dress uniform, and with that, they jumped out of the bed. With them both standing on opposite sides of the bed, they stripped off, pulled back the sheets and blankets, and got back into bed. He was surprised at the pleasure of having her skin next to his and touching her.

It was getting into the early hours of the morning, and Nancy said that she needed to go to the toilet. He knew that she needed more than that and said, "You can shoot up here, I don't mind". Nancy was surprised and got out of bed and went to her bag, pulling out a small bathroom bag.

Jack had read her mind and knew exactly what she wanted, but he wanted to see it. She had heroin with her and prepared it to draw it into a glass syringe with a needle. She offered it to Jack, but he declined while assuring her that it was okay for her to do it.

With that, she put on a tourniquet around the top of her arm, found a vein and injected the heroin into her blood. He was fascinated watching as she got the hit. She packed up the kit and immediately came back to bed, and they fell asleep together.

They woke up in each other's arms the following morning. He was aware that she had an addiction and would need to shoot up again, and assured her that it was okay. Jack rang and ordered breakfast in their room.

He was finding it quite enjoyable being around her. She went to leave mid-morning, and he asked if she'd like to come back that evening with the understanding that he would give her money, and she readily agreed. Jack said to her that she didn't need to wear makeup or her normal attire for her profession, while telling her that she was beautiful without all that.

He even knew that her hair was beautiful in its natural state and said, "Don't go to any effort with your hair, we'll be in bed a lot". Nancy felt shy and said to Jack, "Are you sure?" She returned the following night but without make-up and had her dark hair pulled back into a single hair band, showing how beautiful her blue eyes were and in a modest dress.

He said to her that she looked more beautiful than ever. But then the dress wasn't going to stay on for long, and it was a relief to her not to have to spend an hour on her makeup and hair. They would end up spending the next week together during the night.

Ronnie and Jack caught up for lunch that day, and Jack asked him, "So what is this human sex thing about besides making babies?" Ronnie laughed loudly and replied, "One of the best pleasures in the world".

Ronnie said to Jack that he just needed to let go and experience things at times. Jack could see that he was naive, but he could also see the pain and suffering of human beings around him and was often glad that he did not have to experience that himself.

But he was beginning to see that it also meant he was missing out on experiences in life.

He spent the next few nights just lying in bed with Nancy, talking and sleeping together naked. He sensed that she was falling in love with him and that he was feeling love for her.

It was a new experience, as he knew that he had a love for his mother and some of his relatives.

Jack could even say that there was a love for his father, but it wasn't as strong as the bond he felt towards his mum. What he was feeling about Nancy was similar, but there was something different that he simply couldn't articulate to himself.

On this particular night, Nancy was touching him more than she normally would, and he knew that she was feeling aroused.

He was not feeling anything other than this feeling of affection towards Nancy. She said to him that he just needed to relax and go with the flow, and with that, he allowed himself to let go and feel what she was feeling.

For the first time in his life, he got an erection and couldn't believe how good it felt. She hopped on top of him and slowly let his erection slide inside her. He found her breasts mesmerising, and that added to the sheer pleasure as he had his first kiss with their tongues meeting.

Jack had never felt pleasure like this before as she moved, sliding herself up and down on his erection and the pleasure built until they both had an orgasm together, which literally blew him away. They would go on to make love several more times that night.

For the final few days of Ronnie and Jack's stay, they would spend their day together doing things around Sydney, and then Jack would spend all night making love to Nancy while talking between breaks. On the final night with Nancy, Jack said to her that he would really like to see her again, and they discussed how they could keep in contact. Fortunately, where he was based was probably not more than half an hour away from Kings Cross, where Nancy lived.

Ronnie and Jack returned to base, but Jack could not believe how much he was missing Nancy, but also the experiences that they had at the hotel and in Sydney. Ronnie and he talked about this at length, trying to think about how they could move on in life. But for now, they owed the army three years of their lives, and to walk away from that would mean jail time.

1966 was the year that Australia changed its currency to the dollar, as well as moving from imperial measurements to the metric system. They would both be very busy not only helping to change the maps the army had to the metric system, but also going and training units on the metric system.

Jack would regularly go up to see Nancy, spending a night in a hotel in Kings Cross with her. One night together, after making love into the early hours, they fell asleep. Nancy would sometimes get up and shoot up while he was asleep.

Jack was worried about her heroin addiction that was keeping her bound to her pimp, but he had no real idea how he could help her get away from him. This morning, he woke up and couldn't feel her next to him.

He rolled over, and there she was with her eyes open and her skin blue. He knew straight away that she was dead, and for the first time in his life, he started crying. He sat up in the bed and pulled her over to him. She was cold and lifeless as Jack cradled her, sobbing. He was in complete shock that he'd met such a beautiful person who was now dead in his arms.

He knew about John, who was her pimp and that she had to give him half the money that she earned, as well as that he supplied her with the heroin, even making her pay market price for that. John had hit her several times to instil fear and submission into her as well as for his pleasure.

Jack also knew that she'd had quite a hard life. He was fully aware that she'd been sexually abused as a child and run away to the city, only to find herself in an abusive relationship with a drug addict pimp.

He also knew that John was becoming suspicious and jealous of the amount of time that she was spending with a particular client, and Jack knew full well now that John had given her pure heroin in the hope that she would overdose.

He cried for over half an hour, holding her dead body. Then Jack wondered, just as he could heal his mother's bruises, could he do something for Nancy? He placed one hand on her face and imagined her being alive.

At first, he felt the cold of her skin, but then he could feel glowing warmth under his hand and over several minutes, colour came back to her skin, and she took a deep breath.

Not only had she come back to life, but she had a glow about her that Jack had never seen on her before. The glow that he was seeing was Nancy's skin being a healthy colour and not affected by heroin. Jack had brought her back to life, but also had freed her of her addiction.

Nancy was disoriented and bewildered, and Jack had to explain to her what had happened. She slowly came to this realisation, and as the morning went on, she knew that she'd been dead.

He told her all he knew about John, and she was quite surprised. She was thinking about this and said that there was no way she was going to be able to go back to him, but she had no money. Jack could see the fear in her eyes.

He reassured her that it would all be okay and that he would take care of her, even though he wasn't exactly sure how he was going to do this. He was on a very low wage and knew his savings would run out. They got into a taxi and went down to a motel near the Randwick Barracks, where he paid for her to stay two weeks in advance.

CHAPTER SEVEN

Jack had a conversation with Ronnie about how to resolve the situation. He knew he would have to get John out of Nancy's life. He had a plan and went through it with Ronnie. While on the one hand, Ronnie was surprised, on the other, he wasn't, as he knew Jack was a force to be reckoned with. Jack asked Ronnie to get him a quarter of a pound of the best quality heroin that he could get with a promise he'd get it back.

He knew exactly where John lived in Kings Cross and went there one evening with the bag of heroin. He knocked on John's door, which was answered by one of John's friends and associates.

Jack had learnt enough from reading Nancy's mind to know the names of John's drug dealers. As such, he said to John's associate that he had been told to come there with a product to see if John was interested in buying it.

The associate let Jack in, and he met John in the kitchen. John peppered him with lots of questions as he had a suspicion that Jack might be an undercover police officer. He was able to give him enough answers to satisfy John that he knew all the people that John knew.

John then said, "What have you got to show us?" He pulled out a brown paper bag that had in it the heroin wrapped in aluminium foil and said, "This is some pretty pure shit". John said, "Do you mind if I try some?" This was going to be his way of seeing just how good it was. Jack replied, "No worries".

He took a small amount out of the foil and then made it up into a mix and shot it up. Within 20 seconds, he said, "That is pretty good shit, how much do you want for it?"

Jack gave a figure that Ronnie had told him to, knowing that John would cut the heroin with other stuff. John looked at his associate, who was standing to Jack's right. Jack immediately knew that they would be taking the stuff off him without paying for it. John's friend pulled out a handgun and pointed it at Jack's head.

While remaining seated, Jack grabbed the hand of John's friend with the gun in it with his left hand, quickly pulling him towards him. The gun fired at the floor. He then quickly placed his right hand up behind his friend's head and smashed his face into the table with great force.

Jack stayed sitting at the table with John's friend directly in front of him, unconscious. He then grabbed the man's head with both hands and snapped his neck, with him falling to the floor lifeless at Jack's feet. John was calm in his drug-altered state and had grabbed his handgun and was pointing it straight at Jack, who looked at John and informed him that he was the guy regularly seeing Nancy.

John smiled, pointed the gun at Jack's head and pulled the trigger. The hammer clicked on the bullet, but the gun didn't fire. This was what Jack had hoped would happen, but he still felt an enormous amount of relief that it hadn't fired. Jack got up and walked towards him. John was panicking while continuing to pull the hammer of his pistol back and pulling the trigger, only to have nothing happen.

Jack grabbed the back of John's head by the hair and slammed his head into the table with such force that it partly broke the tabletop

He still had his hand on the back of John's head, and he pulled him back onto the chair that he was sitting on. The front of John's face was completely smashed in, as he was gasping for breath and stopped breathing within 15 seconds. Jack didn't feel anything watching John die except that he'd got the job done that he'd set out to do. He looked at the scene for a while as he had just killed two humans for the first time in his life.

He was surprised about snapping John's friend's neck. But when his father was telling him about the hand-to-hand combat with the Japanese soldiers, what his father didn't say out loud, but Jack could see, was that they went around and snapped the necks of all of the Japanese troops that were still conscious, including even some that were dead.

There was no one else in the house, and Jack knew that there was money and drugs stashed in a safe. He went into John's room, where there was a hidden safe and knew exactly what the numbers were, having read them from John's mind. He opened the safe and in it was over £20,000 in bundles of £50 notes, as well as a one-kilo block of pure heroin.

He found a bag in the room and put it all in there, as well as retrieving the bag of heroin that Ronnie had given him. He decided while he was in the kitchen that he might as well take what money both John and his friend had on them. To his surprise, they both had several hundred dollars' worth of newly minted Australian dollar notes on them. That would cover Nancy's accommodation for the next few months.

Jack had been staying with Nancy at the hotel, but had organised to meet Ronnie somewhere private. He not only gave Ronnie the quarter of a pound of heroin that he'd borrowed from him but also the one-kilo block. Ronnie looked at him, stunned, and Jack said, "You can give me half of what you get for it". Ronnie knew what had gone down and not only had a new respect for his friend, but wished he had been there to see it.

It appeared that they would be staying at the Randwick Barracks for at least some time, plus Nancy would need somewhere to stay when Jack was sent to Vietnam. The £20,000 cash, converted to $40000, was more than enough to buy a home near the barracks with plenty of change left over. Ronnie moved in with them, and they were within walking distance of the barracks.

Nancy loved that she had a house to live in with a partner who she felt would never hurt her. Jack had no expectations of what he wanted from Nancy, except to be with her. She was free to do whatever she wanted.

He gave Nancy $5000 in cash and said that it was a gift from John. Nancy looked at him, baffled, as he said, "John's gone". She knew straight away that Jack had killed him.

She felt both horror and relief as she didn't think that when Jack said that he would take care of her, he would go and kill John and take his money. But she also felt a lot of relief that John was completely gone.

Nancy decided for now that she was quite happy to just be a homebody, and she would spend her days going up to Bondi Beach and other parts of Sydney that she had missed due to her nightlife lifestyle and sleeping all day.

Jack even spent some of the money on buying them a new Ford Falcon car. He never drove it to work as he knew that would raise immediate suspicions with his colleagues as to how he could afford it on an Army private's salary. Not only did the car give Nancy freedom to go about her days, but on the weekends, the three of them would go off exploring Sydney.

Jack was still very keen to learn Kung Fu, and Ronnie took him to meet Huang, who had been Ronnie's teacher. Huang owned a Chinese restaurant in Chinatown where they met him, and Jack had the pleasure of also discovering Chinese cuisine. Huang was nearly twenty years older than them and was a very affable man with a great sense of humour. Huang was about five feet six inches with black hair and a very solid build. He was a second-generation Australian born to Chinese parents and spoke fluent Mandarin, which Jack would come to learn and loved to talk to him in. He knew that Huang did more than own the restaurant.

Ronnie had not said anything to him, but Jack knew that Huang was the drug dealer from whom Ronnie got his stuff, and who Ronnie had sold the 1kg block of heroin for £1000.

Huang owned a very nice home in Surry Hills that was within walking distance from his restaurant. He had a nice courtyard that was set up for teaching karate. He taught his own sort of non-contact Wing Chun and Tai Chi. His philosophy was that there was no need for them to touch each other at risk of hurting themselves, and to save that for those who needed to be hurt. What they did was like a choreographed dance with karate moves and having your body in a very rigid state as it moved, with some moves being quick, using the full force of the body. Jack loved it, and they would go to Huang's house several times a week.

Huang was very impressed with not only how quickly Jack picked up karate, but with his strength. They would do knuckle push-ups, and Jack decided to show off one day by doing one-arm chin-ups, which Huang couldn't do.

Jack's time at the Hilton had given him a taste for money, and he and Ronnie had talked about ways that they could increase their income, given their own very low salaries in the army.

Jack had read Huang's mind and knew that he was having problems sometimes collecting money from some of his dealers, as well as others who were ripping him off. Jack and

Ronnie spoke to Huang about this and agreed that they could help him out at the cost of 10% of what they collected.

They also agreed that should they find anything else while taking care of these matters, they would get to keep it themselves, or in the case of drugs, sell it back to Huang at below price. Huang happily agreed, and just like that, Ronnie and Jack were to have a part-time career as hired thugs.

They were yet to embark on this career, and one evening while the three of them were having dinner together, Nancy said to them both, "When were you gonna tell me about your new jobs?"

Both Ronnie and Jack stopped in mid-chew with their jaws half open. Jack said to Nancy, "How did you know?" She replied, "Do you not think that I can't read minds too?"

Jack spoke to Nancy that night, and she said that she'd felt something change in her the first night after they'd made love. He had been thinking about giving her powers like he had with Ronnie, but had decided to just give her some time to recoup from the changes in her life. Jack did wonder if she had some of these powers when they first made love, then why had the heroin taken her life?

He was coming to realise, just as he experienced the alcohol that night with Ronnie, that there was still a level of mind discipline required with the powers, as to what you allowed and didn't allow and what you're aware of and not aware of.

PART TWO: THE MAKING OF A BOSS

CHAPTER ONE

A section of the troop that Jack and Ronnie were part of was sent to Phuoc Tuy Province in South Vietnam to provide accurate maps and geographical intelligence to the army. They knew it was only going to be a matter of time before either one of them was sent.

Jack was quite keen to go, but he could tell that Ronnie was not feeling like the adventure. He had got a taste again of the Sydney that he loved. He had also started dating a lady he had fallen for, Susan. Jack worked on a plan to get Ronnie out of the army and make some real cash for them both.

Given the nature of their work in the army, they had now become Lance Corporals, though even Jack was starting to think about life outside of the army himself. Ronnie agreed with this, and Jack said to him, "Are you prepared to go to the next level?" Ronnie knew straight away that he was saying, "Are you prepared to kill?"

They met up with Huang at his place with a feast of takeaway food from his restaurant, and Jack, having mastered the art of chopsticks, proceeded to enjoy. He said to Huang mid-meal, "Your problems are bigger than a few people who owe you money or are stealing from you. You have people that are wanting to take over your business?"

Huang never ceased to be surprised at how much Jack knew about his business and was becoming suspicious. Ronnie had assured him that Jack had come from a farm and was not connected to anyone in Sydney. Huang was still suspicious, but an instinct had him feeling that Jack was not a cop or a part of another crime group.

He also felt he had nothing to lose with what they were offering. Huang told them about a particular crime group that had been his competition in Sydney for many years, but that he was being squeezed more and more.

Jack said to Huang, "If we can make this problem go away, how much would that be worth to you?" Huang said to them that he would need to think about it, as he knew that should he take on this crime group, there was the potential for a turf war.

In preparation for the fact that Ronnie and Jack would end up going into people's homes, Jack ran a couple of experiments at their place. He knew that both access and silence were going to be critical. One day, Jack asked Ronnie to go and stand out on the footpath. Jack went and stood in the backyard and yelled out to Ronnie as loudly as he could.

He imagined that the sound was contained within a small space around him. He even yelled out loud that Ronnie was a "fucking cunt". He went back through the house and out the front, where Ronnie was still standing on the footpath.

Ronnie looked at him and said, "What the fuck am I supposed to be doing out here?" Jack laughed and said, "You didn't hear a word that I said did you?"

He then told him what he'd done, and they both had a laugh with Ronnie saying he wanted to give that a go, leaving Jack standing on the footpath. Ronnie returned five minutes later, telling Jack everything that he'd said. Jack, of course, had heard everything Ronnie had said as he had wanted to hear it, but wasn't going to tell him. But he also knew Ronnie had kept what he said in a small bubble around him. He also knew that no one in the neighbourhood had heard either of them.

Jack went down to the shop one evening to get some takeaway food and locked the front door before he left. He knew there would be a noise made when he closed the car door, and even from the squeaky gate that he'd been meaning to fix. Jack imagined they're being no noise being heard by anyone else as he shut the car door and opened the gate.

On approaching the front door, he imagined it unlocking without him having to pull out his keys and placed his hand on the door. He heard the lock unclick and opened the door. He proceeded through the hallway with the squeaky floorboards and onto the kitchen, where Nancy and Ronnie were waiting for him. Jack stepped into the kitchen, and they both jumped out of their skin, as they'd not heard a sound of him coming. Jack was satisfied that he and Ronnie were going to be able to pull off one of the biggest underworld assassinations in Sydney's history.

Knowing that they couldn't be heard by the neighbours, one evening Jack and Ronnie sat out on the back porch with Ronnie drinking beer and Jack enjoying Johnny Walker whiskey on ice, having allowed himself to feel some of the effects of alcohol at times.

They had a long conversation where Jack laid out a plan that would set them up for the future. Jack said that he planned to still go to Vietnam, but that he understood Ronnie didn't want to go. He told him to trust him and that he would work it out so that Ronnie could stay in Sydney.

They had another meeting with Huang, and Jack told him in part what it was that he and Ronnie planned to do. They said to Huang that if they were to pull it off, he had to give them 10% of his earnings over the next twelve months, and as per the previous agreement, Jack and Ronnie would get to keep whatever they found in the house.

Huang couldn't believe what they were planning to do, and what they were offering concerning payment was a very good deal. He readily agreed as he seriously doubted they could pull it off and not get killed themselves in the process. Jack knew that Huang had semi-automatic handguns and asked if they could borrow them with the assurance that they would in no way lead back to him, even though they were black market guns anyhow. Huang gave them these weapons with extra magazines and ammunition.

One day at the base, Ronnie and Jack were having their lunch under a big Moreton Bay Fig tree. Jack pulled out a piece of paper where he'd drawn out the plans for the house they were going to enter and told Ronnie how they were going to go about getting in.

They weren't going to have to worry about security systems as none were in place, but there were several security guards on the grounds. Jack knew that they could move across the ground when the guards were not in certain areas, as he would know where they were, but that they wouldn't hear them anyhow. They simply had to get into the house and to the lounge room where their targets would be.

That night at dinner, Jack told Nancy that he and Ronnie would be borrowing the car at about midnight and wouldn't be back until the early hours of the morning. She knew straight away that they were going to do a job. A part of her wanted to say no, and a part of her wanted to worry, but she just knew that Jack was going to come home safe.

They went to the harbourside suburb of Bellevue Hill, where there was a mansion with sprawling grounds. Jack parked the car on a side road where one of the fences of the mansion was. The fences were double brick and had been topped with cement and broken glass. He had warned Ronnie about this and assured him that they would not need protection as he would make it disappear, and they would not get cut.

They had dressed casually and tucked their handguns in their trousers behind their back. The fence was about nine feet high. Ronnie put his hands together, which Jack put a foot in, and Ronnie helped lever him up to the top, where he straddled the top of the fence, just like they did on the army obstacle courses with high walls.

He put a hand down and pulled Ronnie up to the top, and they both jumped down onto the lawn. He knew no one was looking at them, so they walked casually across the lawn to the house, where there was a kitchen door at the back.

The house had servants, but they were in another area asleep, and they knew that they were making no noise for others to hear, despite them hearing what they were doing. The back door was locked with a deadlock as well, but these immediately unlocked as Jack turned the handle, and they were in the house. They could hear a TV and laughing, and both of them pulled out their handguns. He had assured Ronnie that they were completely safe should anyone point a gun at them and pull the trigger. Ronnie, on the other hand, was not feeling confident about this at all and had his gun up, pointing at wherever he was looking as they had been taught. Jack thought he looked a bit comical with fear on his face, even pointing his gun at things that didn't move.

Jack casually walked into the room where six men were sitting on lounge chairs watching TV. All of them were drinking beer and were quite intoxicated. Everyone that Jack wanted to be together was on those couches, and as soon as they saw him, everything happened very quickly. There was another guy behind a small bar who was grabbing a pump-action shotgun.

Ronnie fired at this guy, hitting him several times in the head. Four of the other men on the lounge chairs were reaching for their guns as Jack raised his and fired a round into each of their heads, killing all four instantly. In the middle of the chairs was a two-seater that had Neddy Smith and Graham "Abo" Henry, who controlled the Smith-Henry crime Group. Jack walked in front of them with his gun pointed at them. He simply stated that they had become a rodent to Huang and delivered a single shot into both of their foreheads, and they immediately went limp. Huang had told him that they were both very Catholic, and Jack asked Ronnie to bring him the pump-action shotgun. Ronnie handed it to him, and Jack said to him, "You may wanna stand back so you don't get blood on those nice clothes". He took a few steps back so that he was about six feet away from them and shot them both in the face with buckshot. He did this knowing that without a face, they would not have an open-coffin wake, which was a message to their crews. Ronnie was shocked at what had happened, but then Jack never ceased to shock him.

Jack told Ronnie to go and get several garbage bags from the kitchen, telling him exactly which cupboards they were in. He stood where he was with the shotgun, taking in the scene and was surprised at just how much blood there was everywhere. He also knew that the other five men who were dead were all top-rank lieutenants and hitmen in the crime group. They were going to be hard to replace in the medium term.

When Ronnie came back to Jack, he told him to follow him, and they made their way down into the wine cellar, where there was a hidden door that was covered up by a wine rack. Jack pulled the wine rack forward, with it crashing on the floor, smashing bottles of fine wine everywhere. Ronnie said, "Do you know how much that wine would be worth?" Jack just shrugged his shoulders. The door was heavily locked with three large padlocks, but each one came off as he put his hand on them, and he opened the door. As they entered the room, there were shelves full of cash.

He could see Ronnie had got two garbage bags and said to him, "I think you should go back and get some more". In all, they hauled out over £200000 in cash as well as five 1kg blocks of pure heroin.

There were guns, gold and other things of value in there, but Jack was pretty happy with what they had and didn't feel like carrying it all out, not to mention the bother of having to sell it.

They got back to the car and put all this in the boot. On driving away, Ronnie said, "That was fuckin' fantastic". Jack said to Ronnie that the night was not over yet. He had added another mission that he hadn't told Ronnie about. They drove on from there to the Lansdowne Hotel in Chippendale and parked the car not far from it.

He had explained to Ronnie what they were going to do. It was now after 2:00 a.m., and the hotel bar and reception were closed. Jack also knew that their targets were in deep sleep. They had to both jump to grab their hands on the bottom of the outside fire escape, as it had a drop-down ladder that was pulled up. They were able to lift themselves easily onto the first-floor level and made their way up to the top floor, where again Jack was able to unlock the door from the outside and enter the corridor. The targets were in separate rooms, and Jack wanted them to be shot in the face with the pump-action shotgun that he'd borrowed from the last job.

There were two guards in the corridor who each received a bullet to the head. Given that no noise was going to carry, Ronnie then opened up the first door and flicked the light on, and Jack entered. The light hadn't woken the target, so he stood at the end of the bed and gave it a bit of a shake with his knee.

The man sat up with a fright, and Jack discharged the shotgun directly into his face. The man fell back, gasping for breath. He was still breathing about fifteen seconds later, and Jack knew that while he was going to die, he didn't know how long it would take.

He went around to his bedside, pulled out his handgun and fired two shots into the dying man's head, and his breathing stopped. He then went to his bedside table, pulled out his wallet, took a key from it, and then put the wallet back into the drawer.

He placed the key in a secure pocket and then repeated the same thing with the second target. Jack had just killed

Barry McCann and Thomas "Tough Tommy" Domican of the McCann-Domican Crime Group.

They took themselves back down the external fire escape. Jack threw the pump-action shotgun into a dumpster bin, knowing there'd be none of his fingerprints on it, and they returned home. He had a shed in the back of the house that had a padlock on it that was hardly a safe. They threw the money and drugs in there, where Jack would take care of it over the coming week.

CHAPTER TWO

Jack and Ronnie went to work the following day, and the killings were the headlines of the afternoon papers. Jack was naively confident that they had made a clean getaway. What he hadn't picked up on was that part of the Smith-Henry crime group's squeeze on Huang was that police who were on Smith's payroll were watching Huang, and were also taking note of the two tall white men who were visiting him. Jack and Ronnie were followed by them, and they knew where they lived and where they worked.

At 2:00 a.m. that night, he was awake and became aware of several people in his street who were going to come and kick down his door. Ronnie was asleep in a room on the opposite side of the house, and Jack woke him up without having to say a word or go and see him. Even Nancy was now awake, and she said, "They're coming for a shakedown". He quickly put on some trousers and a shirt, and he told her to go into the bathroom and stay there. He met Ronnie in the kitchen, and Jack went to the front door as Ronnie instinctively went to the back door. He immediately imagined that any noise that was going to happen was going to be contained within the boundaries of their property, with the neighbours completely unaware of what was happening.

The police officers knocked loudly first, and he immediately opened the door before they kicked it in. The Detective looked surprised that Jack was at the door to greet them and punched him in the face.

He fell to the ground, holding his head, showing pain even though he had felt nothing. He instinctively knew that he had to show the cause and effect of what had happened. The police officer screamed at him to get up.

When they got into the kitchen, Ronnie came through, and one of the officers who had a gun out told him to "stop right there".

Both Ronnie and Jack were placed in handcuffs, with their hands behind their back and made to sit on chairs. The two main antagonists out of the six police officers were Senior Detective Inspector Kelly and Detective Sergeant Krahe.

Jack was very quickly processing what was happening and, like a computer mining data, pulling from their brains all the information that he could. He didn't quite know what Nancy meant when she said it was a shakedown. He now realised that by pulling over the rack of wine in the cellar, he exposed the secure room and the fact that half the contents of that room were missing.

He was annoyed at himself, as he knew he could have put the wine rack back with all the bottles intact. These police officers wanted to know where it was to take for themselves and would leave Nancy, Jack, and Ronnie shot dead if they found the cash. Jack was asked if he killed "Neddy Smith". He said "No", and the detective inspector immediately punched him in the face.

He allowed himself to get a split lip and have blood pouring down his chin and onto his shirt, as he was still trying to work out how he was going to manage the situation.

Jack was communicating with Ronnie and saying to him, "Just go along", and Ronnie received his fair share of questions and punches to the face. He knew that the police were going to rip the place apart and that the shed was still full of all the cash, including the five kilograms of heroin.

He then realised that would mean the police wouldn't kill them, but they'd all get life in prison with their mugshots on the front page of the newspapers. Jack even allowed lumps to form on his face with the several punches that he received and had to admit that Inspector Kelly had a fairly impressive punch. Just as Inspector Kelly was about to tell the others to rip the place apart, Jack said, "I'll show you where the money is". Inspector Kelly grabbed him by the front of his shirt and said to him, "No, you'll tell me where it is". Jack said that it was in a safe that only he could open. Inspector Kelly pulled him out of the chair and said, "Which way?" He replied, "It's under the bed in the bedroom". Inspector Kelly pushed Jack down the hallway to the bedroom.

On getting into the room, the two other officers with them flipped the bed onto its side, only to find that there was nothing underneath it. Immediately, Jack let the handcuffs on his wrists unlock, where they fell off, and he hit Inspector Kelly so hard that it smashed his face, with him falling to the floor, dying. The officer next to him went to grab Jack. He very quickly hit him hard in the head while he was spinning around while doing one of Huang's fancy round kicks, connecting with the other police officer's head, who was pulling out his gun.

He stood there knowing that they still had a situation on their hands with one dead policeman and two unconscious ones who he knew had brain bleeds and would be dead soon. He grabbed the two police officers who were still unconscious and lifted them by their belts with one hand in each. He carried them back to the kitchen, where he also knew that Ronnie had taken care of the three police officers who had waited there.

He threw the two of them on the ground and went back to the bedroom, where he brought Inspector Kelly's dead body back. Ronnie was in a mixed state as on one hand, he had done exactly what Jack had instructed him to do, but on the other knew that they had a major problem on their hands.

Ronnie looked at Jack's face, which was completely normal again, and he had no blood on his shirt, but Ronnie's face was still a mess. Jack walked over to Ronnie and put his hands on Ronnie's face, immediately bringing it back to normal and said to him, "I'll work it out".

The three police officers that Ronnie had hit were still unconscious, but Jack figured, given that three of them were dead, he might as well finish off the other three and immediately went and snapped their necks. Jack knew that Inspector Kelly and the other five police officers had not discussed this visit with any other police officers. But they had mentioned Jack and Ronnie to other colleagues in terms of seeing them with Huang.

He was thinking about ways to dispose of the bodies when he remembered the episode with the branch spinning and flying off into the bush. He picked up Inspector Kelly and took him out into the backyard, knowing full well no one was looking over the fence. Ronnie followed him out and was amazed to see what happened. Jack stood before Inspector Kelly, whose body came off the ground and proceeded to go straight up. Given all the work that Ronnie and Jack were doing on the metric system, he imagined the body going to 300 metres above the ground and just staying there.

He couldn't see the body but instinctively knew it was right where he imagined it to be. He turned around to Ronnie and said, "Let's bring out the other five bodies". They laid them all on the ground, and Jack imagined them with Inspector Kelly's body, and they immediately went off the ground at speed. Where Jack lived was only several kilometres from the ocean, and he imagined all six bodies moving through the air at 300 metres above the ground.

Jack's mind was still like most people at the time, converting from imperial to metric. He commanded the bodies to go to 100 miles per hour, wanting them to be many miles out to sea before he would let go of control of them, and then they would drop into the ocean.

He then did a calculation in kilometres and realised that if he let them go for 20 minutes, they would be at least 50 kilometres out to sea. He looked at his watch and said to Ronnie, "We need to take care of their cars". Jack first went back into the house and saw blood everywhere from bleeding noses and faces.

He stood and imagined it all being as it was before the police officers came, and with that, it was. He then immediately went to the bathroom door and told Nancy that it was okay to come out. He knew that she'd been through shakedowns before with John and that they could be very brutal. He assured Nancy that everything was okay, but that Ronnie and he needed to take care of a couple of things first, and they'd be back within a couple of hours.

With that, Ronnie and Jack put on some shoes and went and found the cars just around the corner of the block from the house. Jack knew Ronnie was going to say, "But we don't have the keys?" At which point Jack imagined both cars started up and unlocked, which they did. He said nothing out loud but communicated to Ronnie that they would take the cars to one of the car parks up in the headlands near Bondi Beach and leave them there.

Ronnie was already aware from the night before that when it came to fingerprints, he didn't need to think about whether he left them, as they didn't leave any. As they were driving, Jack decided that leaving the unmarked cars in a car park would be found quicker than if they just left them parked in a street with lots of other cars. They went to North Bondi, found a street with lots of other cars, parked there, and got out. Ronnie knew full well how they were going to get home, and Jack said with a smile, "It's a nice night for a jog".

They were about seven kilometres from home, so it only took them just under an hour to get back home with a casual jog, as Jack didn't want anyone who saw them to think anything other than they were up and out for an early morning run. Ronnie said to Jack, "Where are the bodies now?"

In the whole process with Ronnie and him yacking during their jog, he had completely forgotten about them. He had assumed that because he had the idea that their bodies would drop into the ocean after twenty minutes, that's what would happen. He looked at his watch, and it had been nearly one and a half hours since he instructed their bodies to be flung at 160 kilometres per hour in an easterly direction.

Jack stopped for a moment and saw that they were still moving with many of them having lost their shirts. Some had even lost their trousers and shoes, given the sheer power of the air pressure against their bodies at that speed. What he thought was a command of them dropping out of the sky had just been an idea, and he hadn't made the command.

Jack then commanded it to stop for them, and could see gravity take over, and their bodies were falling back to earth, even though the atmospheric pressure was slowing them down. It only took a short moment to see them hit the water at over 120 kilometres per hour, over 240 kilometres out to sea.

This wasn't what Jack planned, and he was perplexed. He would learn that there was a difference between thinking about what he could do with his powers and the actual command to make it happen. This was in a way, assuring, as things wouldn't just happen if he were toying with an idea. Jack said to Ronnie, "I think they're well and truly gone". Ronnie laughed out loud and said, "Your dick and Nancy certainly make you not focus at times. I hope one day you don't leave me hanging 300 metres above the ground and then forget about me". They both burst out laughing with tears in their eyes as the whole episode had been very full-on.

Jack assured Nancy again that everything was okay and went to work the following day, where it was front-page news in the afternoon papers that six police officers were missing, with one paper linking it to the assassinations of the underworld figures the night before. When Jack read the news, he said to Ronnie that he needed to go and take care of the loose ends. Ronnie knew exactly what they were, and Jack said that he was going to go to the infirmary, claiming that he had a very bad back from all the work that Ronnie was making him do. Ronnie smiled and said, "I think you're the one making all the extra work for us".

With that, Jack was able to go straight home to be greeted by Nancy, who was holding the afternoon paper. He said that the police officers were never going to be found, and he would be making sure that they were not going to be bothered by the police again. She found it hard to believe him and believed that he could end up dead or in jail. He said that he'd been given several days off due to a "bad back".

Nancy said to him with anger, "I'll give you a fucking bad back". He promised that she could do that to him that night and said, "You can break my back as many times as you want". She sighed and smiled, and they hugged.

He went to see Huang, who had hit the whiskey pretty hard. He said to Jack, "What the fuck have you done?" While holding an afternoon copy of the paper reading about the missing police officers. Jack replied, "I've given you the keys to the city". Huang said, "What about the police? They'll kill me". Jack assured him that they were not going to be a problem and that he would take care of it. He told Huang that he needed something from him, but assured him that it was nothing major. Huang had a fear in his eyes, knowing that Jack could not only kill on demand, but he would kill cops or any other person who got in his way. Jack gave him a piece of paper and said that he needed a driver's licence, unsigned in both names that were on there. Huang was very well connected in Chinatown and said to him,

"How quickly do you need it?"

"As soon as possible"

Huang went and made a phone call and said that he could have it in an hour. Jack replied, "What's for lunch?" During lunch, Jack put a bag up on the table that he had with him and said to Huang, "That's for you if you can give us half of what you get". Huang opened the bag, and there were five one-kilogram blocks of heroin in there. He knew by the symbols and writing on the blocks that not only had it come from the Golden Triangle, but it was from a very top-quality producer with almost 100% purity.

Jack hadn't heard of the Golden Triangle, so Huang educated him on it over Peking Duck and rice wine. He went that afternoon and parked in the central business district of Sydney, and went to the Bank of New South Wales, which had a vault with safety deposit boxes.

When asked what size boxes he wanted, he picked up the bags he'd carried in and said four times the size of these. He filled out the paperwork, paid the rent in cash, and was taken down to the vault where the person with him put one key into a lock of the drawer, and he put the other key into the second lock. There was a table where he could have the two safety deposit boxes he got when the bank employee left him to himself.

He started to fill them with all the cash that they'd got from the night before. The two driver's licences that he got from Huang had the fake names McCann and Domican's had used for their safety deposit boxes, where he had the keys that he had taken from their dead bodies. He hadn't quite worked out how he was going to go about using the licences, particularly if staff members were aware they were McCann and Domican's boxes.

But here was Jack in the room where their boxes were by himself with the keys, and even though he knew that a second key was needed to open the boxes, he would just unlock them himself, even without using the keys he had. While he had his boxes out, he went and got the two boxes of McCann and Domican's.

He was glad that the boxes that he'd got were a lot bigger than he was expecting, as there must have been over £500,000 in total in both their boxes. He quickly transferred the cash into his boxes and placed the others back where they came from, now empty except for the only key that the dead owner would have to open them, left inside.

He couldn't believe that he and Ronnie had made over £700,000 from one night's work, which would equate to over $20 million in today's money. He had no idea what he was going to do with this and would have a discussion with Huang about the best way to move forward with this much cash.

It took the police weeks to find the missing cars, and there was simply no evidence as to how the officers had disappeared, as they hadn't told anyone what they were doing. Though Jack and Ronnie were suspects, as the dead had spoken to other associates about their suspicious behaviour with Huang. The police did call on them at their house with both Jack and Ronnie in uniform.

They simply said they were having Kung Fu lessons with Huang. Jack knew, however, that this was going to be escalated and that they would be arrested, taken in and brutally interrogated. He decided to get ahead of this and knew that the lead detective was going to need what Jack would come to call "A bedside talk".

Jack entered the senior detective's house as quietly as he had the others and went into the bedroom where the detective was asleep with his wife.

He made her go into a deep sleep that was as though she were anaesthetised. She was not going to be aware that he was even in the room. Jack turned on the light, and the detective woke up, startled at first.

He went straight for his bedside table, where his service revolver was and grabbed it. Jack raised his arms into the air but slowly walked towards the detective, who told him to stop. Jack put his hands behind his back, where he had his handgun. He placed his hand on the handle of it as the detective pulled the trigger on his revolver, only to have it click. He continued pulling back on the hammer and pulling the trigger, only to have the cylinder move to the next bullet and nothing happen. Jack pulled out his gun and pointed it directly at the detective's head.

He even let the detective keep his revolver in his hand, saying, "Your guns won't work on me". The detective had his gun tested several days later, and it worked just fine. Jack said that he was there to talk and sat on the end of the bed with his gun casually lowered, but still pointing at the detective's body.

The detective looked at his wife and was surprised that she hadn't woken. Jack replied, "She won't be waking up while I'm here". The detective sat up in bed, stunned that his gun hadn't worked and here was this person sitting on the end of his bed with a gun pointing directly at him.

Jack began to explain to the Detective exactly what he knew about their investigations into the disappearance of the six officers. He was taking information from the detective's head and saying it back to him, but the detective was completely overwhelmed by the amount of information that Jack knew about their investigation. He went on to tell the detective that he knew he was also on the take with McCann and Domican while saying the number of a safety deposit box that he had that contained over $200,000 and the bank that it was in. He then said, "So here's the deal, you will now work for Huang, and you'll continue to get your nice money. But if you don't play nice, you're dead".

But Jack knew this wasn't going to be enough. He went on to name the detective's sons and daughters, describing them, their addresses, their telephone numbers, the places they worked at and even the cars that they drove. He even named his grandchildren and the schools they went to.

Jack then raised his gun and, pointing it directly at the detective's head, said, "If I can kill six armed police officers and make them completely disappear, I can do it to you and anyone else. Do we have an understanding?"

The detective nodded, but Jack added that should any of his officers come back at Jack or any of his associates, Jack would know way beforehand and act first. He stood up and proceeded to say, "I would also have no hesitation killing your mistress", telling the detective her name, address, telephone number, job and car type.

He then fired a bullet into the detective's right shoulder, going through his deltoid muscle. The Detective immediately held the wound while looking at Jack in horror. This was a simple flesh wound, and Jack said, "Just so you know it's not a dream, but no golf for the next month". He turned around, turned the light off and left the house, knowing that the police would leave him and Huang alone for the time being. But he knew full well that they were going to need reminders every now and then, even if it meant the occasional dead cop.

CHAPTER THREE

One morning, Ronnie was asked to go and see their commanding officer, who informed him that he was being transferred immediately to fill a role at headquarters in the CBD for the army, as they urgently needed someone to fill a position who had legal skills.

Ronnie met up with Jack to have lunch under the big Morton Bay Fig tree, as they often did. He was in shock that this was the last day that he was going to be at the Randwick Barracks, not to mention that he and Jack wouldn't be working together anymore for the time being. Jack simply said to him, "Well, you wanted to stay here in Sydney, and it's happened", while smiling at his friend.

Jack and Ronnie were sitting out on the porch that evening when Jack said to Ronnie, "I have something for you". He went into the house and came back out with a thick folder that had "private information" written on it, along with Ronnie's name on the side. He handed it to Ronnie, who realised it was his army records. In it was everything from his enlistment, transfers and anything that related to his time in the army. Ronnie found the sheet that was from his time at Kapooka, and they both laughed at some of the comments that had been made by recruitment instructors about his performance at times. At the very top was the transfer form that said he was being immediately transferred. Then Jack said something that blew him away, "That transfer form has not been received by headquarters, and they know nothing about it. If we burn that file now, there will be no record that you were ever in the army, except for some people you might run into. You're a free man". They went down to the incinerator in the backyard and burnt the whole file while having a beer together.

Ronnie knew that Jack had somehow got into the records room, and not only had he taken his file, but he had somehow intercepted the transfer after their commanding officer had got it, and that Jack himself had instigated the transfer forms.

Ronnie and Jack caught up for dinner one evening at Huang's, and Jack at first spoke to Huang about what he should do with the cash that he had in the safety deposit boxes. Huang gave him the name of a manager who worked at the bank and said to him that he would convert the cash into a bank account for a personal fee, no questions asked.

Jack then spoke to Huang about how he could take over the territory and businesses of the Smith-Henry Crime Group and the McCann-Domican Crime Group. Huang felt that he simply didn't have the resources and firepower to take over their territory. Jack immediately said to him that he would like to buy into the business.

He said that Ronnie was no longer in the army and could work full-time sorting out the organisation of the other crime groups. Huang had been feeling a lot of relief that Jack had taken away his problems overnight. But Huang was also aware that it wouldn't take long for either of the other crime groups to rebuild or for someone else to take over.

What Jack was offering him was a long-term solution, and Jack and Ronnie had proven to be the most effective hitmen in Sydney. Huang's mind then wandered as to how it was going to work financially.

Jack said to him that the business gets split three ways, with Ronnie and Jack owning a third each. He said, "You can keep all the money from the five kilograms of heroin we gave you, don't worry about the 10% of the 12 months' earnings that you owe us, plus I'll give you another $200,000 in cash. I'll also put in $100,000 for capital".

For Huang, the offer was too good to resist, as his current business was modest and Jack was paying more than it was currently worth, not to mention that Jack was promising a large expansion.

He immediately said yes. Huang also knew that it was going to be better to have some white men involved, as there was enormous racism towards the Chinese community that would have worked against him had he become the head of a big crime group in Sydney at that time.

Ronnie immediately went to work with Huang on not only organising the business structure, but also with Huang educating him on many of the ins and outs of the trade of being a successful big-time drug dealer. Huang said to

Ronnie, "This is not the same as handing a bag of shit to your uni friends".

Jack knew they were going to need a much bigger crew. Not only would they need to recruit those who had been working for the other crime groups, but they would need to pull others into line, as well as terminate some who were not going to play ball. Jack spoke to Ronnie and said that Ronnie could impart his powers on others as he saw fit.

Ronnie worried about this and said, "But what if they turn on us?" Jack had given this some thought and had felt that there was a failsafe mechanism within the powers that, as Ronnie had been completely loyal to him, anyone that Ronnie gave the powers to would have loyalty to them. The following decades would prove that it was 100% true and that Jack could revoke it if needed. This was the start of what was to become a very big network that would, in time, span the globe with Jack as the boss.

Jack gave Ronnie half of what was left of the money they got from that night, after he had given Huang the money to buy into the business. Jack hadn't told him about the £500,000 that he'd got out of McCann and Domican's safety deposit boxes, as he wanted it to be a surprise for him. Ronnie bought a nice harbourside mansion in Potts Point that had views across Woolloomooloo Bay. You could also see the Sydney Harbour Bridge, and in time, the newly built Sydney Opera House.

Jack and Nancy would often spend the weekends there as he remained at Randwick Barracks. Nancy had asked him why he was remaining in the army when it was obvious that he was able to get himself out of it. Jack said that he had a greater plan that would set them up for the rest of their lives and that, for now, being in the army was a part of that.

She knew not to doubt him, but she did notice the change in Jack, who was more guarded about what he let her read from his mind. He knew she was thinking this and assured her that it was simply not to overwhelm her with things he had to do or experience.

Infantry battalions were now starting to come to Randwick Barracks to get themselves ready for deployment to Vietnam. Jack was helping to train them on navigation and reconnaissance.

His work impressed his commanding officer, and given that the bulk of Jack's work was with commissioned officers, he jumped a ladder and was promoted to Sergeant. This was also so that he had command over many of the people that he was training.

There were very few Vietnamese people in Australia at this time, but the army had managed to get a person who spoke the language fluently, who would give the battalions basic training on the language for common things that they had to say and ask for.

Jack got to know Lun and asked if he could receive lessons that he was happy to pay for. Jack was completely proficient within one month, even though he could have done it in far less time. He didn't want Lun to be suspicious, even though he was completely impressed at the proficiency that Jack had in the language. Given that Jack was the first white Australian that Lun had come across who spoke Vietnamese so well, they formed a good friendship.

Not only did Jack want to learn more about Vietnamese culture, but Lun wanted to learn about Australian white people's culture. Jack's commanding officer spoke to Lun one day and asked him what he thought about Jack's grasp of the Vietnamese language. Lun said to him, "Just as there are many different accents that you see in the United Kingdom and the United States and slang words, Vietnam also has these things, and Jack has shown to be very adaptable to these quirks in the language".

Jack and Nancy's life flowed along, and Jack was finding that he wasn't having to get involved in the business with Huang and Ronnie doing a very good job. Ronnie was even teaching Huang some of the powers. He laughed at Ronnie one day and said, "No wonder Jack knew so much about my business". Sometimes they would have problems and would come to Jack, but Ronnie had now come to learn that he could talk to Jack at a distance without the need for the telephone.

Jack physically didn't get involved in situations that needed that, but sometimes at night, he would lie in his bed and help guide Ronnie and some of the other hitmen with instructions and intelligence on how to get their target or resolve issues.

This went well into late 1967, and by this time, Jack was receiving a whole year's army salary from the drug trade every week. Ronnie took care of this and set up a proprietary

Limited company in Nancy's name that ran several import businesses, leaving Jack as a humble army Sergeant.

In late 1967, Jack got word that he was to be deployed with the section of his troop and sent to Phuoc Tuy Province, where a section was already there. One of the skills that Jack was the best at in his section was the ability to look at maps of Vietnam and correct them with photos that were being taken by reconnaissance aircraft. Where a Vietnamese map might have a ridge, Jack could see that it was flat and vice versa. Jack's maps were proving to be very accurate.

Nancy wasn't at all surprised that the time had come, and she said to Jack, "I want a baby and to marry you. I need a part of you while you're away". Jack had a stunned look on his face as he discovered Nancy was also able to keep her thoughts to herself. He wasn't expecting this and immediately thought about his birth while his father was overseas.

He could tell that Nancy was upset that he didn't have a spontaneous, excited reaction. He then said to her, "What? In that order? I thought you were supposed to get married first and then have a baby", where she punched him in the shoulder.

Jack had been thinking about how he would have contact with Nancy while he was in Vietnam. He said to her that they would get married, but when it came to having a baby, Nancy had to let him do one thing, "I need to go away for a night to the Blue Mountains by myself". Nancy was perplexed by the request and at first had some suspicion that Jack might be going off to see another woman. But she'd learned enough about Jack to know that he didn't do things without there being some kind of plan, all be there the occasional missteps.

Jack did read this bit of her thoughts and said to her, "I don't always get things right, but I try", and they both laughed. And with that, one Saturday, Jack took the car and left early in the morning. Nancy was getting ready for bed when she heard the front door, and then there was Jack, and they went to bed together and made love. She said to him,

"I thought you were staying away for the night"

"I can't stay away from you"

She ribbed him and said, "How on earth can you go to Vietnam and last one week when you can't last one night without me here?" with them both laughing. They made love again and fell asleep in each other's arms. Nancy woke up the next morning, and he was gone. She went outside, and the car was not there, just as when Jack took it on Saturday morning. That evening, Jack came home. She had made them a nice roast lamb dinner, and while he was eating, she said to him,

"What have you been doing yesterday and today only to come home last night?"

"I stayed the night in the Blue Mountains"

"But you were here last night!"

Jack said with a straight face, "You sure you weren't dreaming that?" Nancy picked up a spoonful of mashed potatoes and flicked it at Jack, hitting him right in the face while saying, "Don't mess with my head". He smiled while wiping his face and said, "Do you remember what I said to you last night about what day we'd get married in a few weeks and that to have a baby, we would have to make love at least three times a night for two weeks?" Nancy just looked at him as Jack said that he had spent last night in a motel bed in the Blue Mountains, and imagined being with her, and it had worked. He said that he wanted to do the test so that he could come home from Vietnam whenever he wanted to be with her and their child.

He then shocked her by saying, "You're going to get pregnant from last night, it's just going to take a month or so for you to find out from a doctor, so we are living in sin given we're not married". He then added that they should still do the two-week sex thing. She scooped up a handful of mashed potatoes and threw them at him. Jack said while wiping mashed potatoes off himself, knowing he was going to have to get changed, "You seem to like me naked". Nancy smirked and said, "I sure do".

CHAPTER FOUR

Nancy and Jack got married a few weeks later at the town hall by a Justice of the Peace, with Ronnie and Susan being the witnesses. Nancy would have loved to have had a full white wedding like many people do. But she knew there was a time constraint with Jack leaving in a few months, and she was simply happy that they were making this commitment. Jack was already committed to her and would have stayed with her regardless, but he knew that Nancy wanted them to be married, and he was happy to oblige. He wore his dress uniform even though Nancy had asked him to get a suit. He said that he couldn't understand why people wore suits with fake shoulder pads in them to make them look bigger and more powerful, as well as wearing a tie that was like a dog leash.

Jack vowed never to own or wear a suit in his entire life. But he had pride in the uniform, particularly now that he had three stripes on the sides. Ronnie, on the other hand, did wear a suit, though it didn't need the shoulder padding given his large, broad shoulders. Jack poked fun at him, saying that he looked just like his father. Ronnie mouthed the words back to Jack, "asshole". They went to a great restaurant in Circular Quay with a view of the Sydney Harbour Bridge.

Here, the four of them enjoyed a silver service meal with fine wines, though Jack had discovered gin and tonics and had quite a few, even allowing himself to get a bit drunk, much to Ronnie's approval. Jack got two weeks' leave, and he and Nancy drove the car up to a seaside town on the Central New South Wales Coast. They spent every day swimming with Jack doing lots of body surfing that Ronnie had taught him at Bondi Beach. This was a very happy time together, and Jack told her that this would be their life one day.

This was a time that had been given to soldiers to go home and visit family, so he felt some guilt at not going back to Queensland. He was writing letters to his mother and father every week and would receive a letter from them at least fortnightly. Jack wanted to spend this time with Nancy, though it was also his current plan to be back in Australia within twelve months.

In a discussion with Ronnie and Susan, Nancy had decided that she would move into the mansion with them when he left to go to Vietnam, as it was now official that she was pregnant. He was happy as they would be around to help, given his trips home would be short.

Ronnie had imparted some of the powers to Susan. In the final month before he left, Jack and Nancy moved into Ronnie's house and sold the house near Randwick Barracks. One night over dinner, Jack explained to Ronnie and Susan that they would still get the see him around every now and then. Ronnie wasn't at all surprised, but Susan said to Jack, "How?" Ronnie replied, "I'll tell you later". That evening, Jack and Ronnie were sitting out on the balcony enjoying the harbour views. Ronnie now had a butler who brought them out drinks and seemed to know just how Jack liked his gin and tonic. Jack said to Ronnie that the police were going to become aware that he had gone to Vietnam and were going to see that as an opening to squeeze money out of them. Jack then said, "Let me know as soon as it happens, and I'll take care of it".

Given that Nancy and Ronnie were fully aware that they would probably be seeing Jack at least a couple of times a week, his going-away affair was not a big deal. Jack simply said goodbye to Nancy and Susan one day while leaving the house with his duffel bag. Ronnie drove Jack down to the Randwick Barracks and dropped him off within walking distance, so no one saw Ronnie himself.

Jack would meet up with his unit, and along with a whole battalion, was bused off to Sydney airport, where they were loaded onto several C-130 transport planes. Their trip from there would be very uncomfortable for most people. The C-130, while pressurised, was very noisy, with uncomfortable seating and had less than half the ground speed of a modern Boeing 737. The trip was to be quite long with refuelling stops.

Jack quite enjoyed this, as a lot of the time he would simply close his eyes and hang out with Nancy or Ronnie. This power was proving to be very good and probably the best of the powers so far. It was during this flight that Jack even experimented with being in more than several places at once.

As they were heading towards Singapore, he spent some time with Nancy at Bondi Beach while catching up with Ronnie in a different part of the city at the same time. He found that he could be aware of what was happening at both locations, but he didn't have to focus arduously on what he had to do at the same time.

When they arrived at Singapore to refuel, as the back of the C-130 was opened, they were hit with an oppressive wall of heat. Jack didn't notice this, but all his colleagues were complaining about it. With the sun on the tarmac, the direct heat must have been close to 50 degrees Celsius with high humidity.

There were a few hundred of them on the plane, and they were allowed to go to a nearby hangar where the temperature was probably 10 degrees less. Jack allowed himself to feel the heat and was very glad that he could switch that off and not feel what his colleagues were complaining about.

They headed off to Saigon, where Jack spent time with Nancy at the beach, swimming and sunbaking. She said to him, "It's as though you haven't even left". He had a broad smile on his face, saying to Nancy that he loved being able to do this while his actual body was stuck on a plane with several hundred sweaty bodies. They landed in Saigon to pick up mail, some supplies and a few people who had been on leave, then onto the Nui Dat base in the Phuoc Tuy Province.

Jack was quite happy to be reunited with several of his friends from the unit who had left the year before. They were given a large canvas tent that was quite spacious, in which ten of them set up their own little spaces. It kind of felt like recruit school in that they weren't going to have a lot of privacy, but they were free to set up their own spaces how they liked.

Vietnam time is four hours behind Sydney, but this proved to be good in that Jack could spend the mornings with Nancy while lying in his bed in Vietnam. Sometimes in the afternoon, he was able to find some quiet time under one of the trees on the base and have a few gin and tonics with Ronnie on the balcony at Sydney Harbour. Ronnie informed Jack that the police had got wind that he'd gone to Vietnam and had come to him and demanded to be paid double the bribes that they were getting. Jack simply said to Ronnie, "The greedy cunts".

One night, while lying in bed in Vietnam, he went to visit the senior detective again. He put his wife into an unconscious state. Jack turned on the light, and the detective immediately sat up. He grabbed his service revolver, pointed it at Jack and started pulling the trigger. The hammer clicked on the revolver several times, only to have the cylinder turn around and not fire a single bullet. Jack sat on the end of his bed again, pulling out his handgun and pointing it at him.

The detective couldn't believe that there was Jack who was supposed to be in Vietnam, now sitting at the end of his bed. The detective did wonder if he was dreaming until Jack fired his handgun. The detective felt the bullet whiz just by the side of his face, making a hole in the wall behind him that would be there after Jack left.

He said that this was no dream and proceeded to say to the detective, "What the fuck is this double money shit?" The detective lied to him and said that he knew nothing about it. Jack then gave the detective very clear dates, times and conversations he'd had with colleagues. The detective knew that Jack knew all about the discussions they'd had about fleecing them of more money now that he was away. Jack was feeling pissed off that he was having to have a conversation again like this, and the detective could see that he was not at all happy. He then shocked the detective by saying, "You were on a pretty good wicket with us with the money we were giving you all, but given this shit, you're now only going to get half of what you were getting for the next twelve months". He then said to the detective, "When you get an opportunity, check your safety deposit box, as all the money's missing. You play nice and take what we give you, and you'll find your money back in your safety deposit box in a few months".

Jack then informed him that two of his colleagues in the drug squad who liked to plant drugs on people had just been killed, shot while asleep in their beds. He added that this behaviour would not be tolerated and that police who did it would have a short life.

Jack had simultaneously done this while being with the detective. He stood up and said to the detective, "If I have to come back here again, it will be to kill you". He then said to the detective, "By the way, check out my file, and just so that you know you're not dreaming again", he pulled up the handgun and fired it into the detective's right shoulder. This time, he hit his shoulder joint, which would give him a permanent injury.

He again left, but left the light on and disappeared after he left the bedroom. The detective rang for an ambulance with his wife now awake in a hysterical state. He was taken to the hospital with a gunshot wound to his shoulder. There, he would be informed that two of his senior colleagues had been killed in their beds, with multiple gunshot wounds. His other colleagues wanted to take Huang and Ronnie into custody immediately and do raids on all their businesses. But the senior detective told them to hold off for now.

The detective told his colleagues to go to Randwick Barracks and find out whether Jack was in Vietnam or not. He also asked them to get his revolver and have it tested to see if it was working with the ammunition that was in it. It was working fine. A couple of weeks later, he went to the safety deposit box and all the money was gone. His colleagues had told him that Jack had been sent to Vietnam one month ago, and there was no way that he could be in the country. The detective asked for the file on Jack, and when it was brought to him, the colleague looked numb as he said, "There's nothing in it". The file they'd built up was several inches thick, and somehow Jack had managed to take the lot. The detective was wondering if his colleagues were working directly for Jack, even though this wasn't the case.

The detective, who still had his arm in a sling, said to his colleagues that they needed to accept the fact that they were going to get half the money for a year, otherwise Jack would kill them all, regardless of where he was or who they were. And so again they were left alone by the police until the inevitable changing of the guard and another shakedown. At this point, Jack had trained Ronnie and Huang on how to deal with these situations, and they were very effective, meaning Jack himself didn't need to take care of them.

PART THREE: THE DRUG LORD

CHAPTER ONE

The role in Vietnam was to help to plan patrols. But given that Jack had done training with some of the infantry battalions that would come through Randwick Barracks, he was instructed to go on patrols, also given that he was an interpreter. The friends that he worked with continued to complain about the heat and the mosquitoes. Jack occasionally allowed himself to feel this, only to quickly switch it off as it was unpleasant.

Sometimes the patrols would take them into villages where they would engage with Vietnamese people who were surprised at how proficient he was in their language. He had the advantage of being able to read their minds and tailor the conversation. Overall, Jack was quickly picking up that they simply were not welcome. He could see that a lot of the soldiers with him at the time were also wondering what the hell they were doing there. The bulk of them were not career soldiers, but conscripts.

It wasn't working out to be the adventure that he had hoped for, as they were not allowed off base unless they were doing a patrol. Jack appreciated that he had the colleagues that he did to share their tent with, but even they got bored. One night, they wanted to go to an area where there was beer and barbecue. Jack was reluctant as he heard they were often brawls at the place, as for drunk Australians in a pub environment, brawls were common.

This one evening, he went with his friends who were sitting at a makeshift bar when Jack was approached by another sergeant, whom he knew immediately wanted to fight. He had learnt in the army that being tall would often make you a target for short men who felt they had to make a point. As the guy became more antagonistic, Jack said to him, "I don't wanna fight you". He turned his back on him and had a sip of his beer, and the guy shoved him in the back of the head.

Jack hit his teeth on the beer bottle and felt quite angry towards the man. He turned around and stood up. He could tell the man was not feeling as confident as he was, as Jack towered over him and was far more muscular, but his mates were watching.

Jack was very mindful of the fact that not only was there a big audience, but he hadn't been able to practise the levels of power to use, as he had often done things with lethal force. He was aware that if he seriously injured the guy, he would be in a lot of trouble with the army. The man pushed him again, and Jack took one step back while just calmly looking at the man. The man said, "Are you a fucking pussy?" Jack blew him a kiss, knowing that would provoke him. The man immediately threw a punch at him, which he blocked and pushed him with his other hand, though the man only went a few steps back while saying to Jack, "You push like a pussy". The man's friends were laughing, and Jack felt some embarrassment as he had meant to push him harder. The man came back with a full-on punch, and Jack pushed him to the ground.

At this point, the man's friends were egging him on. The man got up angry at being pushed to the ground and ran at Jack to throw another punch. He again blocked the punch, then locked the man's arm in a way that pulled him in close as he used his right hand to stick around the man's throat. He slightly lifted him off the ground while applying great pressure to his carotid arteries. The guy was unconscious in under ten seconds, and Jack held him like that for another few seconds before just dropping him on the ground. He said to his friends, "Take him back to your barracks". They looked at him, stunned, and he said firmly, "That's an order", before turning around and sitting back at the bar to continue his beer.

The officer who was in charge of Jack had seen the whole thing and, several weeks later, asked to see him. He came in and saluted the officer, who told him the stand at ease and proceeded to say that he was pretty impressed with Jack's moves a few weeks back.

The officer eventually went on to say that the Special Air Services Regiment (SAS) needed someone with his skills concerning navigation, reconnaissance and particularly the fact that he spoke fluent Vietnamese.

They were in the same base, so it wasn't as though he was being reassigned from his living quarters, but he was being reassigned from the battalion. The officer proceeded to say, "These are a bunch of hard-arse cunts, so watch yourself. You're dismissed".

One of the things that he was going to have to learn in working with the SAS was how to rappel from an Iroquois helicopter. They did this training on base, and he had no problems with it. The captain of the squad also wanted to see Jack's shooting skills and was highly impressed with how he never missed his targets on the range with a handgun. Out of curiosity, the captain took him to the rifle range to see how accurate he was with the handgun. The rifle targets were much further away, and the officer was surprised that he still hit the targets with great accuracy. Jack said to the captain that he preferred to use the handgun over the rifle in a joking way, even though it was the truth.

Part of their patrols was to be dropped off by helicopter, where they would rappel into the jungle and make their way along ridgelines and near hilltops where they could have views of the valley below. If they were to see Viet Cong movements, then they would radio in coordinates, and artillery and if available, American aeroplanes would come in and bomb the positions.

Even though Jack was a sergeant, it was made very clear to him by Sergeant Brown that he was not a sergeant in the SAS squadron and that he was a "lapdog" even to the corporals. He found some of the guys okay to talk with, but in a way, this was the most unpleasant group of people he'd ever hung out with, and he was made to feel like an outsider. One day, on one of their patrols, they came down through a village that they knew was in Viet Cong Territory. They were coming near a farmhouse, and the farmer, who would have been probably in his thirties was about. Jack was ordered to get as much information out of him as he could by Sergeant Brown. He spoke to the farmer, and while he could see that the farmer gave the Viet Cong material help in the form of food, that was all.

He knew the farmer supported the Viet Cong and hated the Americans, to whom he was by proxy. Jack knew that none of the others in the squadron could speak Vietnamese well, other than basic hello and goodbye. He said to the farmer that he sympathised with him and that he too wished that they weren't in his country.

Jack explained to Sergeant Brown that the man didn't know anything about Viet Cong activity in the area, and Sergeant Brown became enraged and was screaming at the farmer in some sort of pigeon language that even the farmer couldn't understand. Jack was trying to explain to Sergeant Brown that the man simply didn't know anything.

Sergeant Brown pulled up his rifle and shot the man while standing less than three feet away from him. The wife and child of the farmer ran out of the house screaming, running towards the farmer, and Sergeant Brown gunned them down as well. Jack said to Sergeant Brown, "What the fuck are you doing?" Sergeant Brown turned around and pointed the rifle directly at Jack. The other soldiers had all taken a defensive stance, where they turned their backs on the under-control situation while pointing their rifles away in case there was danger coming from somewhere else.

But even they were turning their heads around to look at what had happened. Sergeant Brown still had his rifle pointed at Jack, and Jack said for all to hear, "You truly are a sick fuckin' asshole". Sergeant Brown simply smiled at him before lowering his rifle while saying, "The best gooks are dead gooks". He then told the squadron to keep moving, as they could hear the thumping of the Iroquois helicopter blades from a distance that was coming to get them.

Back at the base, Jack had several evenings in his bed where he visited both Ronnie and Nancy. He explained to them that he felt it was time to get out of the army and what he had concluded was a pointless war. It was early 1968, and he would have been due to get out later that year, but he didn't feel like waiting till then. Ronnie knew that Jack was going to be able to make a clean getaway of his choosing.

On this day, a squadron consisting of six, including Jack, rappelled into the jungle. They were to split up into groups of two to make their way up separate ridges, doing reconnaissance with each pair having a radio, and then to rendezvous in a few days on an opposite hill.

Sergeant Brown told Jack that he was coming with him. The three pairs went their separate ways, with Jack and Sergeant Brown going up a particular ridge. But Sergeant Brown took them slightly off course into very thick jungle instead of going directly up the ridgeline. Jack had the machete, and it took them over an hour and a half to make it a few kilometres as the jungle was so thick. In cutting through some particularly thick bush, Jack knew that Sergeant Brown had pulled his handgun out and pointed it at the back of Jack's head.

He heard the click of the hammer, and Jack turned around with the machete in his hand. Sergeant Brown continued to pull his hammer back on his handgun and pull the trigger. But Jack could tell that he was well-trained as he started to pull back the slide to let a bullet go out, meaning that a new bullet would go into the chamber, where he would pull the trigger again. He did this several times while Jack just stood there looking at him, with Jack starting to smile.

Sergeant Brown threw his handgun aside, pulled up his fully automatic rifle, pointed it at Jack and pulled the trigger, only to have nothing happen. Moving back from Jack, he even dropped the magazine out of the rifle and put a new one in, pulled back the load mechanism and proceeded to pull the trigger on the gun again, only to have nothing happen.

While he was doing this, Jack dropped the machete, pulled out his handgun and in a few quick steps lunged towards

Sergeant Brown, grabbing the front of his vest with his left hand. He pulled him around 180 degrees and threw him into the dense bush that Jack had just been cutting. The bush was so thick that Sergeant Brown landed on his back at about a 45-degree angle.

Jack walked over to him and said, "This is for the three people you killed at that village", and proceeded to fire six bullets into Sergeant Brown's head. While he was aware that this was going to happen, he wasn't quite sure what to do from here. When he fired his gun, he ensured that the sound travelled no further than a metre away from him.

He thought about taking a magazine from Sergeant Brown's handgun and swapping it so it would appear he hadn't used his gun. He clicked the magazine release only to find that his magazine was full.

It was standard practice when loading the semiautomatic handgun before going off on patrol to pull back the slide and put a bullet in the chamber, let the slide move forward, gently release the trigger back onto the gun, and then put your magazine in. This meant that not only was there a live round in the chamber, but there were still the thirteen bullets in the magazine. He pulled back the slide, and a bullet flew out, meaning that his gun was exactly as it was when he had loaded it that morning.

Jack was a bit baffled as he'd never encountered this before. He even looked around to see if he could see any of the casings of the bullet shells as he saw them coming out of the handgun when he fired, but he was unable to find any.

He had caught the bullet that had come out of the chamber. With the slide open, he put the bullet back into the chamber and clicked the slide back. He pushed the magazine back into the gun and proceeded to fire fourteen bullets into Sergeant Brown's body. He expected after the fourteenth bullet for the slide to be left open, so that he could drop the magazine out and reload, releasing the slide to reload the chamber with a bullet from the new magazine.

Much to his amazement, even after the fourteenth bullet, the slide did not remain open, and when he dropped the magazine out again, it was still full. Jack simply couldn't believe it, and instead of mutilating Sergeant Brown's body anymore, he fired his gun into the jungle twenty times, only to find that it was still fully loaded. He looked at his handgun for a moment and then placed it back into its holster. He even got down on his hands and knees and could not find a single shell. He'd just found another power. He then looked at Sergeant Brown, who was riddled with twenty bullets, the most he'd ever delivered into a body.

He then tried to imagine Sergeant Brown's body completely disappearing. But it simply didn't happen even after several attempts, so the powers couldn't do this, or he wasn't doing it properly. Jack wasn't about to make Sergeant Brown's body go into the air and go off flying out into the South China Sea when the sky was full of helicopters and planes.

He took a step back by about three metres and simply imagined the jungle going back to the way it was. With that it did, and the jungle was so thick that they were going through, that he could no longer see Sergeant Brown's body. He decided to just leave him there and turned around and started walking back the way they'd come in, imagining the jungle going back to the way it was before he'd cut it with the machete.

He walked for about five minutes and turned around, and the jungle wall was directly behind him, and he knew that the jungle was restoring itself to what it was before they walked through it.

When he got back to where they had rappelled in, he then proceeded up another ridgeline, which was not the original plan. When he got to the top, he decided that he was going to make camp there for at least four nights, during which time he and Sergeant Brown would be deemed missing.

CHAPTER TWO

He set up a nice camp spot with a tarp. There were heavy rainfalls and sometimes thunderstorms every day, but Jack imagined his camp being dry, and it was. He would have been comfortable even if he were wet but somehow found comfort in the dryness of his sleeping space. As he had found in Queensland, "creepy crawlers" would simply leave him alone.

Many of his colleagues complained about how uncomfortable it was in the jungle. They would get leeches and ticks on them as well as having to deal with ants and spiders, plus the heat and humidity. Jack had allowed himself to experience this once and empathised with his colleagues. But he just didn't have to deal with that. Sometimes he would sit out in the pouring rain with no clothes on, which was something that he'd done several times in the pouring rain in Queensland. He allowed himself the experience of having the pleasure of having the water run over him, even sticking out his tongue and letting the freshwater flow over it.

On his second day, he was sitting out in the rain when he could feel a very large creature that was nearby. He got himself into a kneeling position and coaxed the animal to come to him. Then, out of the jungle into the space where he was, came one of the most majestic, beautiful animals he'd ever seen. It was a fully grown male tiger. They had been warned about these animals, and there had been some attacks on soldiers. Jack had no fear, and the animal showed no aggression towards him.

He even asked the animal to come close to him and asked for its permission to pat it. The tiger came up, and Jack was patting it behind its ears, and their foreheads met, and they stayed in that position for fifteen seconds. He was connecting with the tiger just as he did with the horses back home, and the tiger even became playful.

This took him off guard as it moved in front of him and playfully fell onto him. Jack wasn't ready for this, and the whole 250-kilogram animal knocked him to the ground. It then rolled off him, and they continued to play fight. The tiger was even chuffing, which is the equivalent of a domestic cat purr. He knew that just as the horses would not get tired around him or need a drink of water or to eat, he could give the tiger that gift. He invited the tiger to stay with him, even naming him Lan, which was Chinese for "Mountain mist" that they were currently engulfed in.

Lan even lay down with Jack under the tarp that evening, and he was amazed that his body was even longer than his at over two metres. He thought, "You certainly are a big boy". He felt delighted that he'd met him and to have his company. As Lan slept, he went to visit Nancy that night, and while they were lying in bed, he said to her, "You know how you talk about us getting a dog? How would you feel about us having a pet tiger?" She turned to him and said, "What on earth are you talking about?"

"No, I'm serious"

She slapped him on the arm and said, "You certainly have some wild ideas at times". He went on to explain to her that he was currently in the jungle in Vietnam with a tiger that weighed 250 kilograms. She knew straight away that he wasn't kidding and said,

"You're not planning on keeping it?"

"I'd like to"

Nancy replied, "Those things kill people", immediately regretting that she'd said it, given that Jack killed as well. He took no offence as he could understand that what he was saying to her was coming out of left field.

He then said to her that he didn't plan on meeting this tiger, it just happened to be about where he was camping. He also explained that he could see that one day someone would kill the tiger, and that in time, they would be hunted to extinction in Vietnam. He said to her that it felt like he was saving the tiger.

Jack decided to extend his stay in the jungle as not only was he really enjoying the time there, particularly now that Lan was with him, but it was also like having a holiday, and he could go back and visit Nancy and Ronnie. In all, he would spend over a month there, which also allowed him time to work out what he was going to do from there.

Jack had obtained Ronnie's army files, including his police file, while appearing in the rooms where they were and taking them. He had tried to make Sergeant Brown's body disappear, which didn't work. He wondered whether he could make other things disappear though. He knew that if he projected himself, he could take things with him, but this meant having the object on him first, like his clothes, documents or a gun.

One day, sitting under his tarp, he held his handgun and was going to imagine it disappearing and reappearing. He decided that he would unload the gun just in case he shot himself or Lan in the process. As he imagined the gun gone, it disappeared, and then he imagined it reappearing, and there it was, still unloaded. After repeating this several times, he then loaded the gun and repeated the same thing. He then got out from under the tarp and stood up. He warned Lan that he was going to fire the handgun after it had reappeared to make sure that it worked and kept the sound contained. He fired twenty rounds into the jungle with it still fully loaded at the end. He then made the handgun disappear again and imagined it reappearing tucked in the back of his trousers, which it did.

He pulled it out and again fired several shots before tucking it back into the back of his trousers, and then imagined it had disappeared, and it did. Jack was now confident that he didn't need to carry the gun with him as he could make it appear whenever he wanted it, and that it would shoot with no need to reload.

That night, Jack went to the records room for the army in Sydney, where he found his file. Instead of taking it, he just imagined it disappearing, which it did. Jack then came back to the camp and imagined all the paperwork on him that was in Vietnam disappearing. Jack was aware that communications were happening back at the base since he was missing, and imagined all this disappearing when it was being transferred or communicated.

He made the command that all future communications regarding him within the army were to simply disappear without him having to follow it up. He wasn't sure whether this would work, but several years later, he looked into it, and there was no record of him ever being in the army. He knew that he was not going to be able to erase the memory that people had of him, so it most likely would come to light in the future when someone would recognise him. But just like with Ronnie, Jack's time in the army had ceased to exist on record. He was not even listed as missing in action, as those records had disappeared.

Jack hadn't told Ronnie about Lan, but asked if Nancy would like to meet him and that Jack could bring Lan along one afternoon. Jack and Lan projected themselves into Nancy's bedroom, where she was now over three months pregnant with a baby bump.

She could not get over how beautiful Lan was, but also his size. Jack and Nancy hopped onto the bed and encouraged Lan to jump up, only to have the whole bed frame collapse and crash to the floor with a loud bang. Jack hadn't even given thought to what a 250-kilogram tiger was going to do to their bed with both of them on it as well. Next thing, there was a knock on the door from Ronnie asking, "Are you okay in there?" Jack replied, "Yes, you can come in". Ronnie opened the door and said out loud, "What the fuck?" with a fright when he saw Lan. Jack replied, "Ronnie, this is Lan. Lan, meet Ronnie". Ronnie had seen tigers at the Sydney Zoo but couldn't believe that there was one in his home, not to mention that his friend Jack hadn't told him about it. They all went out on the balcony with Nancy, Ronnie and Susan enjoying patting Lan. They then enjoyed the sunset in the evening together, eating oysters with beer.

Jack and Lan spent the night in Sydney with Nancy. With the mattress on the floor, Lan took up half of it with Nancy and Jack cuddling each other on what space was left. She said, "He will get his own bed, won't he?" Jack assured her that he wouldn't be sharing a bed with them in the future. He told her about his plans to get out of Vietnam and that it was going to take him a couple of months to move to his next destination in Southeast Asia. She said, "Why are you not able to just move your body from where it is to where you need to go?" He had been thinking about this but hadn't been game to try the experiment, wondering whether he somehow might get lost completely in the process.

He did say to Nancy that he noticed that there was something different about the experience of where his actual body was to how it was when he projected himself to other places. She said that it felt like he was there in his normal body. He said that he would give it some thought and work out how to try the experiment of moving his body from one place to another.

He did say that he wanted to have the experience of his actual body travelling out of Vietnam into new countries and learning new languages. They discussed when the baby was due, and he assured her that he would be there. Nancy joked to him, "You're not gonna turn up in that bloody dress uniform, are you?" They both laughed, and Jack said, "You go and buy me the clothes you want me to wear, and I'll wear them. Just don't get me a suit". It turned out that she got him some very nice navy-blue polo tops with cargo trousers and some sneakers. Jack wore these in Vietnam, having now made his uniform disappear, though he kept his army boots as they were well-worn in, and he found them comfortable.

Jack had lunch with Ronnie and Huang and discussed with them what his plans were from here. Their business was now the largest importer of heroin and distributor in Sydney. Jack had said to them that it was always best for it not to be a monopoly, but the annoying part of this was that their competitors would always try and muscle in on their turf, resulting in violence.

Jack went on to tell them that they should expand right along the East Coast of Australia, into both Brisbane and Melbourne, and distribute at a street level. He then talked to them about the lucrative markets of the United States of America and Europe, explaining how they could go about trafficking heroin into these countries.

Jack knew that Ronnie and Huang were also dealing in cocaine and Marijuana. Selling marijuana was far more lucrative in the cities, as people simply didn't grow it themselves. Huang explained that he was getting cocaine from a local source coming from South America and that the market there was rapidly growing into the United States. Jack asked Huang if he could find out as much as he could about the South American trade.

Jack had been thinking about what Nancy had said about taking his body to other places without having to leave it lying in one spot, while he projected another one of himself somewhere else. He decided that he would just have to be brave and give it a go someday, but he wanted someone he trusted to be with him. Jack was currently fifty kilometres from the Cambodian border and wanted to make his way through Cambodia and into Thailand. He knew that the Viet Cong used parts of Cambodia that he wanted to move through as a haven to transport weapons and supplies.

Jack was relatively confident that he could make his way through Cambodia by staying out of the Viet Cong's way, but at the same time, he would travel much more easily if he had their support. Jack was going to have to make a bedside visit to a Viet Cong General in Cambodia.

One day, Jack was sitting out in the rain with Lan beside him and closed his eyes and could see where the general was in Cambodia. That evening, Jack had decided to try something new and to visit the general in his dreams.

This went on for over a week, with Jack making the dreams pleasant for the general, with some of them eating and chatting together in Vietnamese or English. While the general was a communist, Jack knew that he was also a Buddhist, and Jack made out that he was some sort of Buddhist Deity and told the General that he was going to visit him with a tiger in his room one night.

The General's room was in a complex underground fortress that would have been impossible for anyone to get into without alerting people. Jack was in the General's room and woke him up, assuring him that everything was okay. The General was unsurprisingly shocked, but at the same time, something about the weeklong meetings in his dreams that were very vivid had prepared him for this moment.

He spent several hours with the General, during which he also gave him a huge cylinder roll of maps of Vietnam that Jack himself had made. He said that these were a gift that he knew would be of great value. They spoke about the war, and even Jack said that there was no way the Americans could win it.

They continued to have these night-time chats when the General asked him if he would like to meet some of his officers. Jack agreed and stated to the General that he would let him know when he was going to appear so that he could warn his officers that this was going to happen.

They gathered in a dining room with a feast in front of them and strict instructions to other soldiers that they were not to be disturbed. Jack appeared with Lan, and one of the officers got up and went to the ground, bowing towards Jack as though he were some sort of Deity. Jack walked over to him and, putting his hand on his shoulder, said that he could stand and go back and sit on his chair.

Jack had come with another cylinder, and the general now had all the detailed topography maps of all of South Vietnam. This was Jack's first time trying Vietnamese cuisine. This meal was dominated by a lot of pork with chicken broth, plus noodles and was very tasty.

Jack then explained that the main goal of the Americans was a war of attrition. And that the best way for them to beat them was to continue doing what they were doing with basic guerrilla warfare, and not to take them on head-to-head on the battlefield unless they felt confident it was on their turf and terms. He knew that the war was already becoming unpopular in the United States and even in Australia, and said to the Vietnamese officers, "Just hang in there and the Americans will pull out". They had dinner like this several times, with one officer asking if Jack spoke English. Given that most of the group spoke a bit of English, they quite enjoyed having conversations in this language.

CHAPTER THREE

Jack was sad to be leaving his home in the jungle, where he'd spent over a month, which had been a great time. Jack and Lan spent three days travelling through the night to get over the Cambodian border, where they were met on a track by one of the Generals' officers and six Viet Cong soldiers. As had been discussed, the officer and the Viet Cong soldiers would travel with Jack through the jungles of Cambodia and onto Phnom Penh.

Just as Jack had been able to get the maps, he'd also been able to get cash from Nancy, and he handed them all a bundle of $US1000 as well as some Cambodian money. He told them that he wanted them to enjoy the trip and that on getting to Phnom Penh, he would give them more money. They proceeded for nearly twenty kilometres north along a track till it was felt that they could make an easier route to the west, and here they set up camp for a couple of nights.

Lan even went hunting and got them a wild boar, where his reward was a leg of the beast. Jack said to them that they weren't going to have to worry about meat for the trip and that pork would be on the menu every now and then for breakfast, lunch, and dinner.

Heading west, sometimes they would be on tracks, other times they would have to hack their way through the jungle, and on occasion would have the luxury of a rural road. Jack quite liked the group and decided to instil a bit of the powers into them, particularly in not getting tired, thirsty or feeling the discomfits of the jungle and camping. They all commented on this, and Jack knew that they had a belief that he was some kind of Buddhist Deity. Jack felt that at this time he would let them believe that, even though he felt very uncomfortable about it, because he certainly didn't believe it.

One day, as they were on a road, they were approached by ten armed men with their rifles raised, who Jack immediately knew were part of a militia who were going to rob them. He communicated to all the soldiers with him to simply lay their arms down and let him take care of the situation.

As they were approached by the leader of the militia, the leader said in Cambodian for them to give them everything that they had. Jack replied in Cambodian, "We need everything that we have, so we have nothing to give you".

Of course, the leader was not at all happy about this and screamed, "Give me everything that you have". Several of the guns were pointed at Lan. Jack knew that Lan wanted to attack the leader, but instead of commanding him to do it, Jack permitted him to do it.

The leader had been pointing his gun at Jack. Lan lunged at the leader so quickly that when he pulled the trigger on his rifle, he was halfway over with the gun firing into the air. The other men were pulling the triggers on their guns only to have nothing happen.

In the meantime, their leader was screaming as Lan proceeded to maul him to death. Jack had to admit that it was even a bit brutal for him and called Lan off. He went up to the leader, who was half-dead, pulled out his handgun and shot him in the head.

He then picked up the dead man and threw him into the ditch. In the meantime, all the other men who had been with the militia leader were running into the jungle away from Jack. He tucked the handgun into the back of his trousers and turned around to his group and said, "Let's keep going".

The officer in Jack's group was called Phan but liked to be called Sam. He was taller than the other soldiers at a lanky five feet ten inches and wore glasses that Jack had never seen on a soldier.

That night, Sam said to him, "I did not realise you were armed". Jack pulled the Browning 9mm handgun out of the back of his trousers and handed it to Sam and said to him, "As a bonus, if you get me to Phnom Penh, I'll give you that one". Sam admired the handgun before handing it back to Jack, who tucked it into the back of his trousers where it promptly disappeared.

It turned out that Sam had been going to university in Bangkok, living with relatives there before the war broke out, studying accounting and law. He felt it was his duty to return home, even though Jack could tell that it wasn't where he wanted to be.

During their time in Cambodia, Sam was able to teach Jack how to speak Thai. It was a bonding experience for them all as it took them nearly a month to get from the Vietnamese border to Phnom Penh. Jack knew he was not going to be able to walk into Phnom Penh with a massive tiger by his side and seven armed Viet Cong soldiers.

He communicated to Lan about staying in some jungle, but not only would Jack visit him, but as soon as he had himself established in Bangkok, Jack would come and get him. To the others, he explained that they were going to have to walk into the capital as tourists. Jack even got them Thai passports that had a stamp in them from them leaving Thailand Airport and flying to Phnom Penh, and said that they would have no problems crossing the border into Thailand.

Jack then told them to give him a moment. He returned shortly holding seven small backpacks that all had civilian clothes for them that looked like what he was wearing. They all got changed, and Jack said they looked like a tourist group, before explaining that they would have to leave all their weapons in the jungle with Lan.

They understandably were reluctant to do this until Jack, for the first time, pulled out two handguns from behind his back with one in each hand and holding them outward, said, "I have these, so we'll be okay".

When they got the Phnom Penh, Jack could see that there was tension building in the country and that it wasn't a place that he wanted to stay. He spoke to the other soldiers who had been with him, and Sam and two others expressed the wish to continue with Jack to Thailand. He gave all of them another $US1000, and four of the soldiers voiced that they would be happy to stay in Phnom Penh. Jack told them that there was going to be a civil war in the country in the coming years and that it was best that they get out, suggesting that they go to northern Thailand. He told them that he would stay in touch.

Jack had got himself an Australian passport in his name that had been stamped departure from Australia to Bangkok, then on to Phnom Penh. They got a plane, and none of them had any problems at the Bangkok Airport going through customs except for Jack, who had his bags completely searched, including a strip search, while being peppered with questions about why he had been in Cambodia. Saying he'd gone as a tourist wasn't working as he had very little money on him, which was a bit of an oversight on his part after organising everyone else.

He knew he could make money appear, but also knew they'd take it right off him. After they didn't find anything of value, they were still looking for ways to fleece him or send him to jail.

The head officer had formed the view that he was a heroin trafficker and decided that they would plant heroin on him and throw him to the police in the hope someone would get some money out of him. They had taken him to a locked room, and Jack said to each of the two customs officers in Thai, "Will a couple of hundred baht make you happy?" They both looked at him as he pulled a wad of hundred baht notes out of his pocket and threw five notes in front of each officer on the table.

They looked stunned as they had just thoroughly searched him. They then said to him, "We'll take the whole lot". Jack put the money back into his pocket and pulled his handgun out of the back of his trousers. Pointing it at them, he said, "You missed this as well, but be assured, I won't be missing you with it", while pulling back the hammer.

The officers sat there, wondering how they even missed that. Jack said, "You got your money, now I'm leaving".

Putting the gun back, he picked up his backpack and left, even though the door was locked from the inside, which baffled the officers more, as not only had it been relocked on him going out, but their keys weren't working, leaving them to bang on the door for help. He left them in a sound bubble where their banging was not heard for two hours, and he had long left the airport.

After they got let out of the room, they proceeded to write a detailed report with a black mark against his name to never be let back into the country on his immigration papers, as well as to take him into custody should he leave.

This report was filed and disappeared, leaving just the information that he had entered the country. They also wrote a report that was sent to the police to have Jack arrested, but the police never received it, as it went missing in transit.

Jack wouldn't fly on an aeroplane again for over 10 years, but was confident that he could manipulate immigration files.

It didn't take Jack long to fall in love with Thailand, and he knew that he wanted to have a house here. He arranged for Nancy to wire him money, and he went about buying a home that was a large old-style timber home in Bangkok that needed some love but was on a large block of land. Sam and the two soldiers stayed with him in the home as Jack went about getting Lan. He was right where Jack left him a few weeks before, and they sat and played while Jack explained to him that he was going to take him from where he was to Bangkok. This was to be a new experiment for Jack, as he had not moved a living being in this way. Lan would become the first experiment in this, and Jack knew that he was also going to have to give it a go himself at some point.

Given that Jack's real body was at the house in Bangkok, he sat with Lan and imagined him gone to Bangkok. Lan disappeared from the jungle and reappeared in the house. The part of Jack that was in the jungle with Lan, saw him disappear and knew that Lan reappeared back in Bangkok, and he returned to his body.

Jack imparted more powers onto Sam, who then taught the other two soldiers, Liem and Duy, how to speak fluent Thai.

Both were very keen on fixing the house. Jack gave them money to do so, as well as to employ any other tradesman as they needed.

Jack had told Sam that he would give him his handgun in Phnom Penh, but Sam had decided he'd wait till they got to Thailand, so he didn't have to worry about having it on him going through immigration. He went through the whole routine with Sam in making the gun disappear and reappear, and just like that, Sam had the same ability that he did with the handgun. Sam was becoming a very good friend and was aware of how Jack had brought Lan from the jungle in Cambodia to the house in Thailand. Jack explained to Sam that he could project himself to other places, but his body would always be in the original place and that he wanted to do exactly what he did with Lan. He had wanted to leave this till Nancy was about given an overriding fear that he would get lost in the process.

He spoke to Sam and asked if he would help participate in the experiment by simply having to watch Jack, but to call out for him in his mind if he didn't return on time. He hoped that if he got lost, Sam calling out for him might guide him back. Jack had a housekeeper who was also a fantastic cook.

On this day, he asked her if she would be able to make them a feast that night of his favourite dishes, and if she gave him a list of ingredients, he would go to the markets and get it for her.

Jack explained to Sam what was going to happen and to watch him as he stood in the corner of the room, giving Sam a time that he would be back. With that, Jack imagined himself going and turning up in a very quiet alley where no one could see him. He appeared there just as he would if he were lying in bed and projected himself to a place. He was not far from the markets and proceeded to go and buy all the ingredients that he'd been given on his cooks' list. He even enjoyed some street food in the process and then, after an hour and a half, went back to a quiet place where he knew no one could see him and simply disappeared, returning to the corner from which he'd left the house.

Jack appeared with his backpack and bags of goods with Sam standing in front of him with a very excited look on his face. Sam said to him that he had watched him disappear, then he had gone away and done a few things, then came back at the exact time Jack had told him to. He said, "You've just reappeared with bags of food. You did it!"

That evening, they all sat down to a shared feast of Thai food and rice, including the cook and celebrated what had been a nice day. Only Sam and Jack were aware of what had happened. Later that evening, when he was lying in bed, he decided to go and visit Nancy and took his physical body with him. Nancy was getting very pregnant and was very happy to see him as it had been nearly a week. He explained to her that he had tried the experiment and that there was no physical body in Bangkok at this time. Nancy said she couldn't tell the difference. Jack said, "You'll simply have to believe me, but I can do it". He found that he would take his actual body to more places now, as it felt better than projecting himself. Though projecting himself still had its uses.

He was feeling very settled in Bangkok while frequently returning to Australia and avoiding immigration and planes. Nancy was getting very close to giving birth, and he felt like it was a time to just let things flow along as a new change was coming.

Jack and Ronnie were having a discussion one night when Jack told him that he wanted to take the next step in the drug trafficking trade, but that he'd wait until the baby was born. He said that he'd be aware when Nancy went into labour, but asked Ronnie if he could be about as well and to have some of his bodyguards at the hospital.

CHAPTER FOUR

It was late 1968, and the time had come. Nancy had gone into labour. This was in the evening in Australia, and Jack was still in Bangkok at the house. It was in the afternoon there, and he said to Sam that he had to go, but to just call out if he needed him. With that, he disappeared in front of Sam.

He appeared at the house with Nancy, and he and Ronnie assisted her to the car to take her to the hospital as planned. At the hospital, they were met by two of Ronnie's associates who had very impressive physiques and were almost as tall as Jack. He knew that not only did they have the powers, but as he had shown Ronnie, Ronnie had shown them how to have a firearm on them, which was completely concealed.

He wasn't expecting trouble from any of their enemies, but from the hospital itself. They were led by a staff member up a corridor near where the birthing suites were. He told Ronnie's two associates to stand at the start of the corridor, and Ronnie proceeded with Jack and Nancy up to what was called the case room.

There, they were greeted by a nurse and midwife, and they went through the paperwork. Nancy was having the occasional contraction but was doing quite well. At this point, a middle-aged male doctor walked in and told both Ronnie and Jack that they were not supposed to be there. Jack stood up and put out his hand to shake the doctor's hand, who refused. Jack said, "I'll be staying with my wife thanks", with no aggression but with absolute authority. The doctor immediately became irate, demanding that they leave. Jack replied, "I think you're the one who's gonna have to leave".

The doctor stormed out of the room to go and find security. Jack had warned Ronnie that this was going to happen, and Ronnie had assured him that he would take care of it and left the room himself, leaving Jack with the nurse and midwife. He could tell that the nurse and midwife were a bit scared of him, but he simply assured them that he just wanted to be with his wife during the birth. The midwife, whose name was Kathy, had a firm belief that the husband should be present, but knew the doctor would put a stop to it. Jack pulled out a wad of $50 notes and gave them each two hundred dollars while saying, "We'll all get through this together. I've helped give birth to calves before", while pretending to roll up a long shirt sleeve he didn't have, in which they all burst out laughing.

He stayed with Nancy as her contractions were getting closer together. Kathy said that she was doing well, encouraging her to push during contractions. Down the corridor, Ronnie and his two associates had simply refused the security guards' entry into the area, which was near the door to where Nancy, Jack and the nurses were.

There had been some pushing and shoving, but the security guards knew they were going to get out shoved. The security guards went away and called the police, and within about twenty minutes, two cars arrived with four police officers. As they approached Ronnie, they knew who he was and knew that he was a very dangerous man in the Sydney drug trade.

Ronnie was quite polite with them and explained to them that his boss was with his wife while she was giving birth. The police were aware of who Jack was and were curious to see him. One police officer went as far as to say, "If we could just talk to your boss, we should be able to sort this out".

Jack remained with Nancy but projected himself so that he was coming out the door, and went down to where Ronnie and the four police officers were.

While the police officers didn't show it, there was a sense of awe and fear that they were getting to see the famous Jack Armstrong, who was known amongst police as the head of the biggest drug crime group in Sydney, but also a notorious cop killer who couldn't be brought to justice.

Jack shook their hands and thanked them for their time while explaining to them that he was going to be with his wife for the birth, regardless of what the doctor wanted. He then encouraged them into the corridor a bit more so that they could not be seen by other staff and proceeded to hand each one of them $200 in cash, which was nearly a month's wages each. Jack said to them, "That should be the end of this matter" and walked off back to the door.

The police looked at Ronnie, who just shook his shoulders and said to them, "It's best that you leave him to be with his wife, I'd hate to see him angry at this time". The police left, and Ronnie could see that they spoke to the doctor, with the doctor becoming quite animated before the police walked out the door, hopped in their cars and drove off. Jack and Nancy would never see that doctor again during their visit.

The labour went along perfectly, and the baby was born and placed onto Nancy's stomach at her request. Kathy was reluctant about this at first, as the procedure was that the baby was to be taken, cleaned up, then wrapped up and given back to the mother. But Kathy knew both Nancy and Jack were the ones in charge, plus this was another hospital rule she disagreed with. Nancy was crying with joy while Jack was touching the baby.

One of the decisions that both Nancy and Jack made was that they didn't want to know what the sex of the baby was, and for it to be a surprise. The technology wasn't available at that time for them to know, but they both knew that they could know if they wanted to and had decided to simply switch that off. Throughout the whole process of the baby lying belly first on Nancy's belly, neither of them had even thought about the baby's sex until after five minutes. Jack asked Kathy, and she replied, "You have a baby daughter". Jack and Nancy had decided on names for whether it was a boy or a girl, and as such, she would be called Michelle. Jack loved this and the fact that the baby had dark hair just like her mum.

At the time, it was standard to stay in the hospital for at least a week, but both Jack and Nancy were feeling impatient. Jack offered Kathy double her salary to come and be with them, and Nancy discharged herself from the hospital against medical advice, though the doctor was probably happy to see them go.

Susan also loved having a baby in the house, and Ronnie was seeing where that was going to lead. Jack stayed for about two weeks until Nancy said that she was getting sick of him being around and told him to "go off and do some work". He laughed and said, "You can't just keep her to yourself".

He had dinner with Ronnie and Huang to celebrate the birth of Nancy and Jack's child. Huang already had three children, with some in high school. Ronnie and Huang were buying their drugs wholesale from Sydney dealers. Jack planned to buy the drugs directly from the producers and bring them in themselves.

This would be the perfect plan, as it would cut out a lot of money in paying the traffickers, not to mention the fact that the heroin and cocaine they bought were cut to about 50% purity, meaning there was more money to be made there as well. Jack had taught Ronnie and Huang how to project themselves to other places, and he suggested that they visit his house in Bangkok, where they could make some plans from there. A time was made for the following week, and Jack returned home to Nancy to annoy her some more while enjoying his beautiful daughter.

The following week, Huang and Ronnie turned up at the house in Bangkok. They met Sam, and Jack gave them a tour of the house and the land that was now being tended to by two gardeners. There was still a lot of work to be done on the place, but both Ronnie and Huang were impressed and could see the potential for it to be a very beautiful house.

That evening, Ronnie, Huang and Sam sat down with Jack, and they had a shared meal with Thai beer. They knew that Jack having Sam there meant that not only had he given him the powers, but that he was a trusted part of Jack's life.

He laid out the plan and said that he'd already made enquiries to meet with a drug lord in the Golden Triangle. If everything went to plan, then he was hoping to get about 200 kilograms of pure heroin a month from the drug lord.

He had created a rumour mill in Burma in the area where the drug lord was, that two white men were seeking to do business with him and that they had money.

Jack and Ronnie were at the house in Bangkok, and Huang was back in Australia. He said to Ronnie that it was good they were not going to have to trek through the jungle for weeks, with him not having to listen to Ronnie complaining about the heat and mosquitoes.

They both smiled at each other and then appeared near a track that was less than half an hour's walk away from where the drug lord was located.

They both had large backpacks that had tents and food, which made out that they had been trekking for quite some time. On getting to the compound where the drug lord was, they were stopped by armed guards holding AK-47s and fully searched.

Jack had not made a point to learn the language but was discovering that he could talk to people in their language by simply reading their minds, and they're being some natural translation within him being told in his mind how to reply to them in their language.

The guards were quite impressed with the fact that he spoke their style of Burmese. After the backpacks and bodies had been fully searched, a few guards stayed with them while a couple of others went to see whether the drug lord would see them.

A couple of guards reappeared, and they were taken through the compound and brought before the drug lord, Khun Sa. As was a hierarchy at the time, Khun Sa sat in an area that was one foot above the floor, and both Jack and Ronnie sat on the lower floor in front of him with their legs crossed, while green tea was served. Khun Sa had a man sitting next to him whom Jack took an immediate dislike to. Jack could tell that this man wanted to take over Khun Sa's business. The irony was not missed by Jack that he had an AK-47 sitting on his lap with the barrel pointing at Khun Sa, even though he didn't have his finger on the trigger.

Jack was surprised at the lack of gun safety, but that Khun Sa also allowed the disrespect. Jack could tell Khun Sa was aware that this man was at some point going to try and kill him, and Khun Sa had already planned to take him out himself. Khun Sa spoke perfect English and proceeded to talk to them in that language, which his associate sitting next to him didn't know how to speak or understand.

Jack explained to Khun Sa that they were keen to do business with him, and Jack said to him that it was his understanding that one kilo of heroin cost $US500 from him.

He said that for them to make a deal, he was happy to pay $US750 and that for this visit, he would like to buy 10 kilograms. Jack asked for permission to reach into his bag and proceeded to pull out $US7,500 in bundles of $100 notes. He did this and commented to Khun Sa on the discipline of his guards in not taking any of this money when they were checking his bag. He then surprised Khun Sa by saying, "If this deal works, I'll come back in a month with some more men and get 100 kilograms off you with the view to getting that fortnightly". Khun Sa was curious as to who Jack was, though he had heard rumours. In reading his mind, Jack explained to him that he was a major distributor of heroin in Australia and was looking to expand into the United States and Europe. Khun Sa said,

"You are the boss of that, and yet you come all the way here?"

"I wish to show you my respect and how serious I am about getting this deal done"

Khun Sa raised a cup of tea, and with the motion of a toast, they raised them, and Khun Sa said, "You have a deal", and they shook hands.

He then said to Khun Sa in English, "You have a problem with the man sitting next to you, I would like to offer you a gift". Khun Sa simply nodded his head, and Jack pulled a handgun out of the back of his trousers and shot the man in the head, killing him while immediately putting his handgun back in his trousers. The guards raised their guns at Jack, but Khun Sa lifted his hands and told them to put them back down. Khun Sa then said to Jack in English, "You are a man to be respected. Thank you very much for what you have just done. He was becoming a problem so to speak". Khun Sa ordered some of his guards to drag away the associate and get rid of his body.

They were brought ten one-kilogram blocks of heroin and put five blocks each into their backpacks. Jack said that he would be back in one month, where he'd have a pack horse and probably about four other men with him, and for $US75,000, he would get 100 kilos of heroin from Khun Sa. He thanked Khun Sa for his time and said that he looked forward to catching up in a month, and gave him a date and approximate time that they would arrive.

Jack and Ronnie proceeded back down the track that they'd come up. After walking for about forty minutes, he said to Ronnie that it was time for them to head into the jungle.

There was some light banter between them as Jack ribbed him by saying, "Are you sure if you are ready for this?"

He then got out a machete and took several swipes, but only after taking a few steps in, he turned around to Ronnie and said, "Maybe you should go first, that way you get bitten by the snakes". While Ronnie was laughing, he also knew that he was in an environment that he'd never been in his life.

He was very glad he was with Jack, as on the way up, he had inadvertently allowed himself to feel the overwhelming humidity and heat of the jungle and even the mosquitoes until Jack told him to just turn it off, which he did.

They hacked their way through the jungle for about half an hour until they came to a slight clearing under a big tree. Jack cut down a few plants to make a bit of space for them. As planned, Ronnie had communicated with Huang in Sydney, who was currently in a room at one of their import businesses.

They then stacked the 10 kilograms of heroin on the ground, and Jack stood before it and imagined it disappearing and reappearing on the table that Huang was standing before in Sydney. Huang was surprised when it appeared, as he doubted that it was going to work.

He knew that in a month, he would not only have to make more space on the table, but also make sure that it could hold the weight of 100 kilograms of heroin that was going to appear. Huang was well aware of how monumental this was, as one of the major inconveniences, risks and costs of being in the drug trade was getting it from its source to where it needed to be distributed. Up until now, they had been getting this from other traffickers, but they were having to pay a premium for the pleasure. Huang knew, as well as Jack and Ronnie, that if they could bring blocks of pure heroin from Burma to Australia like this, then they were going to be able to do it into Europe and the United States. Jack had come up with the perfect answer, which was also going to make them a lot of money.

Jack had kept in touch with the four Viet Cong soldiers who had made their way to northern Thailand and were staying in Chang Rai. He told them about a job of collecting heroin in Burma and proceeded to show them how to project themselves, so that they could arrive about an hour's walk from Khun Sa's compound.

He went through the whole routine with them and explained that they would be paid the equivalent of one year's salary in Thailand for about ten hours of work a month. They had all become keen fishermen and loved the idea that they could go off and work in Burma for a few hours a fortnight and spend the rest of their time fishing.

One of the men organised a pack horse, and along with Jack and the four men, they all disappeared and reappeared on the track about an hour's walk from Khun Sa. They were greeted at the front by armed guards who were much more friendly this time and took them straight through to Khun Sa, who came out to meet them all. Khun Sa invited Jack in to where he had a lunch set up, and they sat down together. Jack gave Khun Sa $US75,000 for the 100 kilos of heroin that were currently being loaded onto the pack horse.

Jack said to Khun Sa that business was picking up quite a bit, and would he be happy if he sent his men up in a fortnight to get another hundred kilos? He said that he would be with them, and Khun Sa agreed, and for the rest of the decade, Jack would have lunch with Khun Sa in Burma every few weeks. They would even share gossip and intelligence about the heroin trade. Khun Sa loved to hear about where his heroin was being sold around the world, and Jack was happy to oblige.

They proceeded back down the track for about an hour, and Jack decided it was time to head into the jungle, where they made their way for about half an hour till Jack found a very small clearing. They unloaded the 100 kilograms of heroin, and then Jack instructed his four colleagues and the horse to disappear back to North Thailand while handing them several thousand Baht each.

He then communicated with Huang in Sydney, and with that, the 100 kilograms of heroin disappeared in front of him and reappeared before Huang, with Jack appearing next to him pretty much straight after. Huang said to Jack that he couldn't believe they were able to do this, and they were going to need a lot more. Jack said at this stage that they could get a couple of hundred kilos a month and take it from there. While Jack was with Huang, they made the 100 kilograms disappear, knowing that it was going to different places up and down the East Coast of Australia, as well as into Europe and the United States of America, where it would be cut and sold. Some was even held in "storage" in their minds, which even further reduced the risk of being caught.

CHAPTER FIVE

Jack, Ronnie and Huang had a meeting at Huang's place a few days after they'd had the successful transfer of the heroin. Huang had made inquiries into the South American trade and believed that Jack would be able to get cocaine directly from a drug cartel in Colombia. He went on to say that the trafficking side of things into the United States was becoming very messy in Mexico, and that they should stay completely out of it.

Jack re-explained to them the importance of not having a monopoly on the market around distribution, but he could see that they could sell more in the wholesale market. As part of the experiment, Huang had already sold several kilos of heroin in Brisbane and Melbourne that Jack had got from Burma for a nice profit. All three of them had participated in transferring the heroin from one place to another by simply making it disappear and reappear.

They had also experimented with a mock raid and had any drugs, cash, or anything else involved in that part of the business disappear, as well as having it reappear. Both Ronnie and Huang had done a great job at delegating to people underneath them, thus reducing their workload.

Huang was feeling more comfortable running the operations in Sydney and felt that he could also set it up on the east coast of Australia. He said that there was currently no room for them in Melbourne, but that the main crime group wanted to sell their business.

Jack asked how much it was, and Huang replied $60 million. Ronnie said, "That's a bit steep". Huang said that he'd seen their books and that they were making a $10 million profit per year. He said, "They are also offering to help with both police and their crew members for at least two years while we get involved". Ronnie stated that it was too much, but Huang added, "There is something powerful about this group that would mean we would have to go to war. I feel like it's a good offer". Jack thought for a moment and then said, "You're confident that they won't fuck with us on the deal?" Huang replied, "They are very well connected with politicians and the police. I think it's a good offer without lots of bloodshed, not to mention their network is impressive. We won't have to do much to be up and running". Jack looked at Ronnie, who nodded, and Jack said, "Buy it". Jack said that he would do the work on getting the product and asked Ronnie if he would like to look at having them make a market in Europe and the United States. Ronnie happily agreed with excitement.

Life continued without any issues into the early 1970s. Jack had picked up that Ronnie and Susan were not very happy together and had a chat with Nancy about it one night. She had not yet been to Thailand, where he had based himself. They had toyed with the idea of Nancy and Michelle coming to Thailand. Nancy had a reluctance to be in a developing country with Michelle as a baby. But at this point, Michelle was over two years old and was proving to be very resilient. She was just like her father in that she never got sick and never got a scratch or a bruise.

Nancy had commented that she wasn't spending as much time with Susan and even said one day, "It's like she's become a bitch". On the other hand, the midwife Kathy had become quite close friends with Nancy and was becoming a valued member of their family. Nancy did say to Jack that she didn't feel comfortable with her body reappearing in Thailand, including that of Michelle's, at this time.

Jack understood this as he remembered his reluctance, and Michelle was not at an age where she was going to be deciding to do that. He then suggested that Nancy, Michelle and Kathy fly across to Thailand and stay for a couple of weeks. She agreed to this, and Jack said that he would get it all sorted with passports and flights.

She then said to Jack that she was not comfortable owning the company that was in her name, as she knew the bulk of the profits were coming from illicit drug sales. He had assured her that nothing that was happening within the company would in any way come back to her. But Nancy still insisted that she wanted the company transferred to Jack.

The company was now worth about a hundred million dollars with an income of ten million dollars per year. Jack had no problem with the company being transferred to him, but he wanted Nancy to feel that she had some financial independence. He asked her if she would like him to pay her out, but she simply replied, "Don't be silly". He then said, "I could buy you the Coca-Cola Company?" She simply rolled her eyes and said, "Just so long as you give me some pocket money, I'll be happy". Jack replied by saying, "Will I need to take out a loan for that?" where he received his mandatory punch in the arm from her.

Nancy, Kathy and Michelle flew first class to Bangkok, and they were picked up at the airport by Jack and Sam and driven in two separate cars back to the residence that Jack had bought. Both Nancy and Kathy could not get over the chaos of driving, as the only road rule appeared to be that there weren't any.

They were both relieved once they got to the residence and loved the house and the gardens. Nancy had shown Kathy how to shut off the impressive humidity and heat, but it didn't seem to faze Michelle at all, and Nancy even noticed how the mosquitoes didn't go near Michelle.

Nancy very quickly came to see why Jack loved the place so much. Using the powers, Sam was able to teach Nancy and Kathy how to speak the language very quickly. This meant that they were able to get out and enjoy Bangkok more without the barrier of the language. Because the household was getting bigger, not to mention the house itself, Jack had employed extra staff. Both the cooks and housekeepers had children of their own and would often bring them over. Sometimes the noise got to Jack, and he quite enjoyed going off to work at times. At the same time, Jack had said to Nancy that he wanted to spend at least a day a week with just him and Michelle.

He loved these days, and while he would spend most of the day around the house with Michelle, he sometimes would take her for a walk in a sling that one of his housekeepers had shown him how to make with a shawl. Nancy came to like it as well, as she would have a whole day to herself.

Back in Sydney with Nancy, Jack and Michelle not around, Ronnie was feeling he had gotten to the point that he could no longer be with Susan. She was pressuring him to get married as well as to have a baby, but Ronnie simply didn't want that at this time.

She was also complaining about the outdated state of the house that they lived in and was demanding more spending money and expensive cars. Ronnie had known Susan at university, and she also came from a wealthy family. She even made it clear to Ronnie that she disapproved of the way that he was making money and that she wanted him to get out of it and make a real living. Ronnie said to her that there was no way he could make the money that he was making being some pencil pusher. During one of their arguments, Ronnie suggested to her that maybe she needed to go and find herself the husband that she wanted.

One night, they were sitting out on the balcony, and Susan became quite intoxicated. She again voiced her disapproval at how Ronnie earned a living, even going as far as to say, "Why do you have a farm boy as a boss?" Ronnie, who had also had a few drinks, went red with anger but calmly said to Susan,

"Do you remember reading about the eleven underworld people who were killed over four years ago?"

"Yes"

"I was present when they were all killed, including killing one of them myself"

Susan looked at him with horror and said,

"Who killed the others?"

"You work it out"

"Jack?"

"Do you remember the six police officers who went missing the following day? I was also present when they were killed"

Susan just looked at Ronnie and didn't say anything as she knew that Jack had been the one who had killed them. Ronnie then said to Susan, "We would not be in this house or be getting the money that we have if it wasn't for Jack, so I think you should show him some respect". She replied that she had no intention of showing respect to some country boy hick and his wife, who hadn't even been to high school.

Ronnie then reached into his pocket and pulled out a bundle of $50 notes that was $5000 in total. At that point, two of Ronnie's bodyguards stepped out onto the balcony, and Ronnie said to Susan, "Take the money, pack your bags and go back to mummy and daddy". Susan hadn't expected this and started to beg Ronnie, who stood up and walked away.

She got up to run towards him, and one of the bodyguards stood in the way and simply said, "You've heard what he said, you need to pack your bags". Ronnie left the place himself and went for quite a long walk, and she was gone by the time he got home. Jack came to visit Ronnie the following evening, knowing what had happened. He was aware of the tensions and was also aware of how Susan felt about him and Nancy, but it simply didn't bother him. Ronnie said to Jack that when he was out walking, he had decided to take the powers that Susan had away from her.

Ronnie said he had no idea whether this had worked or not, but Jack said he had a feeling that it had. Ronnie had not delegated a lot of powers to Susan. As Ronnie and Jack enjoyed a drink along with the mandatory oysters, Ronnie said that he felt relieved while admiring the relationship his friend had. He asked Jack,

"How do you do it?"

"We talk, we listen, we compromise, and we use humour where I sometimes have to receive an almighty punch in the shoulder for stirring her"

Jack did ask, "Did you give her money? When Ronnie said "$5000", Jack showed disapproval, saying, "$5000 for three years?" Ronnie replied that "She was a bitch and was lucky she got that". This didn't sit comfortably with Jack, and he even had a feeling that it could come back to bite Ronnie. But given the culture of the time, he let it go, which he would later regret for not making Ronnie fix it.

Ronnie said to Jack, "This place feels like it's a home for us all", adding that Nancy, Jack and Michelle would forever be welcome there. He thanked Ronnie for that and said that he would certainly take him up on that offer, as Jack had come to love the place himself. He told Ronnie that he'd been talking to Sam about setting up a law and accounting firm in Sydney with the view to that being the headquarters of a worldwide organisation. A problem Jack, Ronnie and Huang were having was that they were making so much money in cash that they needed to diversify that into more legitimate businesses. But they needed a more industrial way to launder it, and Sam had shown a great interest in this. Jack then asked if Ronnie would be happy if Sam stayed at his place at times while he set that up. Ronnie happily replied, "Of course".

The following day, Jack, Ronnie and Huang met up, and Jack shared with them some more of the information that he was discovering about the American cocaine trade. As Jack had investigated it more, he agreed that it was best to stay away from the Mexican cartels and all the trafficking that was happening in that area. He felt that the way forward was to offer one of the bigger cartels in Colombia a way of getting cocaine into the United States completely undetected and then taking a 40% cut of the wholesale price in the US. He knew they'd be able to get cocaine into Australia and Europe in the same way by using the powers. He could see the shift that was coming over the following decades in Western countries, where authorities were going to pour a lot more money into trying to stop the drug trade. He felt that them not controlling all the distribution at a street level and even not controlling all the trafficking would leave enough crumbs for the authorities to pick up without impacting their business.

Jack even went as far as to say to them that they should give the police strategic tip-offs on rivals, as the police were going to want something to show for their efforts. He was certainly not naive enough to know that they weren't going to come to the authorities' attention, as they were already paying a lot in bribes to police officers.

As Jack looked more at the cocaine trade in South America, he could see that it was very disorganised and that now was not the right time to be getting involved. According to Huang, they were getting enough pure cocaine to sell on the east coast of Australia, which was not a big market at the time in the early 1970s. He felt that he'd let things settle for a few years, as they were certainly making enough money from heroin.

CHAPTER SIX

It had been over six months since Ronnie had split up with Susan, and early one morning at 4:00 a.m., there was loud banging on the front of his door, and the house was raided. Ronnie didn't mind having a bit of marijuana and even cocaine at times, and while the police were searching, he'd made sure all of it had disappeared. But the police planted several grams of heroin and cocaine in one of his drawers. The lead detective, Inspector Wilson, was very excited about this "find", as this was going to mean several years in jail for Ronnie.

Ronnie was handcuffed and taken to an interview room at the King's Cross police station. Ronnie had been aware that Detective Wilson wanted to make a name for himself, and that the best way to do that was to get a big fish. Ronnie understood he could project himself out of the police station, but he felt he needed to wait to see what Jack had to say. The police kept him there for days using sleep deprivation, which did not affect Ronnie. At one point, a police officer got so angry that Ronnie was not giving them the information they wanted that he got up and punched Ronnie in the face. Ronnie wasn't going to give him the pleasure, and the bones in the policeman's hand shattered, as hitting Ronnie's face was like hitting a brick wall.

Ronnie didn't get to see that policeman again, and none of the others even contemplated hitting him after it. Detector Wilson had made it very clear that they had got information from Susan and was saying to Ronnie, "You give me Jack, and I can help you get out of here quicker".

Ronnie simply replied, "You have me, but you won't be getting Jack". Detective Wilson told him not to worry about that, as he knew Jack had killed the police officers as well as the heads of the two crime groups. Ronnie was charged with possession of illegal substances as well as one count of murder and sent to Long Bay prison without bail to await trial.

Ronnie had been in touch with Jack and knew to expect him that night. Ronnie's bed was fixed in a corner, and he had no roommate. He sat up at the pillow end. Jack appeared in the room with a medium-sized backpack and sat down at the end of the bed.

Ronnie sat with his back against the wall at the head of the bed, with them at a 90-degree angle to each other. Ronnie was very apologetic, but Jack assured him that it was fine, as it was going to happen to one of them one day. Ronnie told Jack that Susan had spoken to the police, which Jack was already aware of. Jack knew it was in the back of Ronnie's mind that Jack might kill him. He said, "Don't worry yourself about that, not only are you my best friend, but you're very valuable to our business together".

He then opened the backpack and proceeded to pull out a wooden board and make up a platter with Camembert cheese, chicken liver pâté, Prosciutto and olives. He then hauled out a couple of bottles of very fine French wine and said to Ronnie, "I need to make up to you for all those bottles of fine wine that I smashed getting into that room at the mansion". He knew that none of the noise that they were making was going outside of Ronnie's room. He let the lights come on in Ronnie's room, knowing that that was not being seen outside either.

Jack was also aware that the guards didn't check on the inmates at night while they had their long naps. He opened a bottle of wine, and they toasted to Ronnie being in prison. Jack apologised that he couldn't bring beer and oysters as neither of them had learnt how to shuck them, plus the beer would have taken up too much space. Ronnie looked at the platter while holding a glass of wine and said, "I'm not complaining". They proceeded to enjoy the wine and platter while Ronnie was waiting to hear what Jack had to say about the best way forward. They chatted for at least 30 minutes before Jack brought up the topic. He said that the police were not going to get away with planting the drugs and that the evidence was going to disappear along with the cop who planted it. Jack was also confident that if they were going to go through the full process, he could have Susan deemed an unreliable witness, tamper with the jury, and Ronnie would hopefully be set free.

The problem with this was that Ronnie could end up spending upwards of more than nine months in jail. He then said in response to what Ronnie was thinking, "If you make yourself simply disappear, then you'll be a fugitive and will not be able to live your life as freely as you want". Ronnie knew what the other option was and simply said, "I can't kill her".

Jack had another cracker with some pâté, followed by a sip of wine and said to Ronnie, "I certainly won't kill her if you don't want me to". He then added, "Obviously, spending over nine months in here will be relatively easy given that we can catch up whenever we want". Ronnie said, "And the other option?". Jack replied, "I can have you out of here in under a week". Ronnie sculled down what was left in his wine glass and held it out to Jack, who filled it back up and said to Jack in a sombre way, "Do what you need to do".

Not only was Susan bitter at Ronnie, but she found it very demeaning to be back at her parents' house, financially dependent on them, particularly with her mum pressuring her to find someone to get married to. It was in this headspace that she decided to go to the police and told them all that she knew about Ronnie and Jack and their activities. This was done with the view that she would be paid $200,000 and put into the witness protection program with a nice yearly payment.

Detective Wilson was feeling very confident that once Ronnie was convicted to years in jail, he would do some sort of plea deal so Detective Wilson could get Jack. It was

Detective Wilson's associate who planted the drugs without him knowing, but at the same time, Detective Wilson was over the moon that they'd found drugs in the house.

Detective Wilson was aware that there was a high chance that Jack was going to visit him, as he had been told by a previous detective about Jack appearing in his bedroom. He set up a duress button under his pillow and had four detectives living in his house who could be in his room in minutes should Jack appear.

The night after Jack had seen Ronnie, Detective Wilson woke up with the light on in the room and Jack sitting on the end of his bed with a gun pointing directly at him. Detective Wilson was pressing his duress button when Jack said, "I wouldn't bother, it's not working". Detective Wilson's handgun was on the bedside table, but he simply didn't have time to grab it, and he felt that Jack would shoot him should he even attempt to reach for it.

Jack read his mind and fired several shots at the handgun, making it crash off the table. Detective Wilson could not believe that his colleagues had not come into the room after hearing that. Jack replied, "They're not going to hear anything while I'm here". He said that he knew who had planted the drugs in Ronnie's home and that that person was now lying in their bed, dead. He then told Detective Wilson that he knew he didn't know about the planting of the drugs, otherwise he'd be dead too. Jack went on to say, "I know you have kept tapes and documents of your interviews with Susan with multiple copies spread across the city, but tomorrow you're going to find that there is no evidence at all". He then stood up and fired three shots just above the detective's head into the wall and disappeared.

In under a minute, four police officers came into the Detective's room with their guns drawn, with Jack having allowed them to hear the three shots. Detective Wilson told them all to leave the room with him, as it was now a crime scene. He then told them what had happened, and his phone rang. He was informed that the police with Susan had heard a gunshot in her room, where they were keeping Susan and that she was dead from a single gunshot to the head. Detective Wilson immediately sent some of the officers to his colleague's house, and they rang him back within an hour to say that he was dead in his bed with gunshot wounds to the head and chest.

The following day, Detective Wilson went to multiple places where they kept the tapes and files on Ronnie, only to find that they were all missing. He even went to the evidence room where the cocaine and marijuana were kept, but even that was gone. Detective Wilson now had no evidence on Ronnie except for what he and his colleagues had seen and heard, but he knew this would not hold up in a court of law.

Later that day, the forensic team got back to him and said there was no evidence of any gunpowder residue, fingerprints or even bullets in his bedroom.

They then added to everyone's horror that there were no bullets or casings at both the dead police officers' house and

Susan's room. X-rays of the bodies showed no bullets or fragments. Detective Wilson simply could not believe them. He'd even sent detectives to immigration only to find that Jack was in Thailand.

That night, he was woken up again by Jack. Jack said to him, "You have found no ballistic evidence from what happened last night and all the evidence that you have on Ronnie is gone. He then said, "I expect all charges to be dropped on Ronnie tomorrow, otherwise you'll be dead by tomorrow night". Jack disappeared in front of him.

The following day, Detective Wilson had a meeting with several of his colleagues as well as the prosecutor. The prosecutor was very clear that there simply was no evidence to continue with the prosecution of Ronnie. Detective Wilson did say to everyone that he wanted them to write down everything that they had experienced over the last few months, as it seemed that Jack's trademark was that there was no evidence, and they needed to start making some sort of case based on this if they could, not to mention that he seemed like a ghost.

The charges against Ronnie were dropped that day, and he was released from prison. He got a cab back to his place, where Jack met him on the balcony. Ronnie's butler had shucked some oysters, and Jack had beer ready on ice and said to Ronnie, "Welcome home".

Jack allowed himself to relax and become intoxicated with his friend. There was a slight sobering feeling with them however, because Susan had been killed. Ronnie talked about how they were made to be like robots in the army and to kill on order.

He even added that in their business, there was a "kill or be killed" mentality. Ronnie had certainly done his fair share of killing people, but he noticed that Jack was very decisive and could not only make the decision to kill someone very quickly, but also execute it without hesitation.

Susan had been Ronnie's girlfriend for nearly three years, and while he felt very happy that they had broken up, there had still been a love for her. Jack was hearing what Ronnie was saying as well as what he was feeling, then Ronnie asked, "How can you be so decisive and not have it affect you?" Jack had tried not to give it much thought, but then told Ronnie about what his father was like towards him, leading up to the event where his father pulled the trigger on a loaded gun pointed at his head.

This was not something Jack had told Ronnie about. He went on to add that there were no vets available where they lived, and if farm animals became sick, no matter how attached to them you were, then they would be put down with a rifle shot to the head. His father started to make Jack do this from the age of ten. He then went on to explain how he would shoot crows and even feral pigs that took from their livelihood.

He simply said it was just something that he got used to doing, and now he did it with humans. He said to Ronnie that it is a very brutal world, and from Jack's point of view, Susan stepped into the firing line when she went to the police, whom he considered to be their enemy.

Then Jack had some firm words of advice for Ronnie that made him sober up. He said, "Given that Susan was with you for three years, you should have given her several million dollars. Kicking her out with just $5000 was not a wise move, and she probably wouldn't have gone to the police if you had financially taken care of her. Plus, you also may want to keep things about our business to yourself and not tell your girlfriends while you're drunk".

Ronnie had a fear of Jack when he was arrested, knowing Jack would know everything that he had told Susan in the haze of alcohol that night. He could see his actions in how he split with Susan while angry, and kicking her out with little money, led to her death.

He reminded himself that Jack had said that he wouldn't kill her if Ronnie didn't want that. Ronnie made that call based on getting out of jail early, and could even see that Jack could have left Susan for Ronnie to sort out. He could see that Jack had cleaned up a mess that he had created. He saw that he needed to be smarter in the future, as Jack might not be so kind towards him.

CHAPTER SEVEN

Ronnie alerted Jack that an urgent telex had arrived for him at his house in Sydney. Jack was in Bangkok, and he imagined the telex in his hand and opened it

It was from his brother in Queensland informing him that his mother had died in an accident. He had been thinking about going home to visit, but was too caught up in the world that he was living in. His mum was in her early fifties, and he simply couldn't believe that she was dead. Jack's mind was spinning, and he said to Nancy that he needed to go and lie down. She asked him if he was okay, but he just continued and lay down on the bed.

She sat down next to him, and he handed her the telex. He had often spoken about his mum, and Nancy knew that he loved her very much. Jack started to cry, and Nancy lay down next to him, holding him as she'd never seen him cry before. Even Michelle had come in, wondering what was wrong with Daddy, and he hugged her, saying he was okay, and she went off to play. Jack knew that Nancy was worrying as he slowly stopped crying, and he held her closer, saying, "I have cried like this before when I held your dead body in my arms".

With this, Nancy started to cry, saying she could never show Jack how grateful she was that he had saved her. He replied that he was also grateful that he was able to do it, otherwise they wouldn't be lying together now and have a beautiful daughter. But he was already feeling that he was not going to be able to save his mum the same way. It was simply too late, and his mum had none of the powers.

Jack couldn't bring himself to go to the funeral and said to Nancy he would go to his mother's grave in a few weeks. He was able to express to Nancy the guilt that he felt in not going home to visit his mother. He even expressed that he felt he had been selfish in enjoying Nancy and Michelle and not taking them home to see his family. Nancy was very pragmatic over the following weeks as she constantly reminded Jack that families are very complex, even going as far as to say sometimes people simply don't get on. He said that he should have given his mum the powers that he had, but Nancy said to him, "You had no idea at that time that you could do that". For these few weeks, she was the rock that held Jack together. She had never seen him so vulnerable and not thinking straight.

Two weeks later, he stood at the end of his mum's grave in the pouring rain. He spoke out loud to her and found this to be quite soothing. He again began to cry with rain running over his face. He simply said to his mum that he was so sorry and that he should have somehow protected her.

Later that evening, he drove a car to the farmhouse where his father was by himself. The dogs were barking, and Jack knew that they could be quite vicious, but he simply conveyed to them that they were safe with him as he got out of the car, with them jumping on him, wagging their tails. His father turned on an outside light and came out, and was surprised to see Jack. The last letter that he had written to them had been from Bangkok, and Jack said to his dad that it had taken some time for him to get home. He could tell that his father had been drinking, and his father invited him inside for a beer.

They shook hands, as hugging was not something that his father did. His father offered him a beer, and they sat down at the kitchen table opposite each other. They spoke about the farm and the weather, as well as the crops, and everything was going well. Jack had already made inquiries and had seen the police report on how his mum had died, and decided that he wasn't going to ask his father about what happened, but he had read his father's mind.

After about an hour of drinking beer and even reminiscing a bit, Jack said to his father, "Why did you start hitting Mum again?" His father froze and then denied it. Jack looked at his father and said, "You know you can't bullshit me". He then said, "I'm aware that you were both up having your annual holidays on the Sunshine Coast when an argument broke out between you two. I'm also fully aware that you slapped her in the face and she left the apartment, but then you followed her and as she started to go down the stairs you shoved her". He continued, "You then followed her down to the bottom of the stairs where she was severely injured, and you snapped her neck".

Jack's father lowered his eyes as everything that Jack had said was true. With that, Jack shoved the table into his father with such force that his father's body hit the wall behind him and the force of the table hitting him crushed his chest.

He immediately got up and walked around to his father and threw the kitchen table away while grabbing him by the shirt with his left hand. He lifted his father slightly and with his right fist, struck his father so hard in the face that it caved in. This one punch would have killed his father, but he hit him several more times out of anger, with blood splattering on the wall before dropping him to the ground. Jack stood above his father and watched him take his last breath. He then left the house and drove away, making both the car and himself disappear. On paper, he'd never been in Australia, and no one saw him except his now-dead father.

He returned to Bangkok, where it was before midnight, appearing in bed with Nancy, leaving her to sleep while he lay awake with tears in his eyes, hearing Ronnie say, "How can you be so decisive and not have it affect you?". Jack started to wonder whether he was just like his father, who had killed his mum without giving it a second thought.

When Nancy awoke the following morning, she asked Jack how things had gone back in Queensland. He said to her, "How about we go and have a picnic?" About half an hour's walk from where they lived was a large park, and they walked there holding hands, making light conversation. It was a weekday, and the park was not too busy. They found a nice big shaded tree where Jack sat down leaning against it, and Nancy sat down between his legs with her back leaning against him. Jack had bought a backpack and said that he wanted to surprise Nancy while saying that he had done the same thing with Ronnie while he was in jail. Nancy laughed and said, "The things that you two get up to". He almost stumbled on his speech when she said this, as he knew his visit to Ronnie had led to him killing Susan. He didn't know how Nancy would react to it if she knew, and he wasn't about to tell her. He regretted having mentioned that he had done this with Ronnie.

He pulled out things, including the timber chopping board out of the bag, handing them to Nancy, who set it up in front of her, which consisted of cheeses, crackers and fresh fruits, which they both discovered was a very nice combination. They enjoyed having a feed with some bottled sparkling mineral water. She then said to Jack, "Do you want to tell me how it was in Queensland?" He said that it was ugly and said to her, "Do you really wanna know?" Jack had his knees pulled up with his arms resting on them. She put her cheek against his arm and said, "I wanna help you through this". He said to her, "It was not very pretty, and there are some violent things that I've done in my life that I've not told you about". She was already aware of this and was starting to wonder if Jack bottling it up was affecting him.

He told her about visiting his mother's grave in the pouring rain before going and confronting his father. Jack told Nancy about his father pushing his mum down the stairs, which killed her, without going into detail. She said,

"How did your father react to that?"

"I killed him"

She froze momentarily while she processed what Jack was saying to her. He went on to say that he knew that his father had hit his mum when he was a child, before telling her about the night when his father laid into his mother and the incident with the shotgun. He said that after that, for the next ten years, his father did not lay a finger on his mother. He started to cry and said to Nancy, "I guess that's why I'm feeling that I let her down, by not protecting her after I left". Jack wrapped his arms around Nancy, and she put her hands on his arms. She couldn't think of what to say as it certainly explained why Jack was feeling so tormented. They held each other for a while until Jack said, "Let's have some more cheese and fruit".

He then asked her if she minded him having a month off and just staying in Thailand. Nancy said, "Of course you can, that's not something you need to ask me". He said that he would still need to make his fortnightly trip up to Burma. She said,

"Can't you even give that a break for a month?"

"Khun Sa's cooks make one of the best pork dishes I've ever had"

He added that it was all very civilised considering what they were doing, before adding it was only for a few hours a fortnight. Nancy banged her head back into Jack's upper chest while saying, "I knew you'd always leave me for a nice pork dish". They laughed and enjoyed their spot in the park. After about fifteen minutes of sitting there, Jack knew that Nancy was not protecting her thoughts from him and knew exactly what she was about to say,

"I wish you'd kill my father"

Jack said while holding her, "My father just killed my mother, and I've just killed my father. You need to let me have a bit of time to get over this". He then said to her that he would look into it at some point.

Nancy knew full well that when Jack said this, he was either going to get someone to look into a situation and gather every bit of necessary information or do it himself.

She felt some relief that at least Jack was going to look into how it was going back at her home, where she had run away from her father and was wondering about her mum and brother.

Jack enjoyed his time with Michelle, but even at the age of six, she still needed a lot of guidance. Kathy was homeschooling her, with Nancy helping, and Jack was amazed at the amount of knowledge that she was absorbing. He was still surprised that sometimes he would need to be firm with her, as she would play up like any six-year-old would. One day, she was playing with Lan and pulled on his whiskers hard, hurting him. He turned around his head and growled at her while knocking her over. Jack was sitting on the verandah and saw it happen. Michelle jumped up, screaming and ran towards him. He picked her up and explained that she needed to be gentle with animals and carried her back over to Lan, where Jack sat down in front of Lan with Michelle on his lap. He patted Lan's head and rubbed behind his ears while encouraging Michelle to do the same while saying, "Just be gentle".

Michelle would spend time with Liem and Duy, wanting to help them while they were building things. They would be very careful with things that she did, and sometimes gave her a piece of timber with some big nails to hammer into it. They even taught her Vietnamese, and she would talk in that language when she was around them. Michelle would even hang out with the cooks, helping them with food and baking. What didn't go unnoticed by the staff was when she would hit her hand and even once got boiling water on her hand, but was not injured.

Jack was guiding her through the powers that she had, and sometimes she would sit in the garden, making sticks come to her or sit in the air, having them spin about. Jack knew that there were rumours amongst the staff about Jack being a Buddhist Deity, as was his daughter. He also knew those rumours would spread.

Nancy had gotten into Theravada Buddhism and had some of the books, which she encouraged Jack to read. He had read a couple of versions of the Bible and found it to be the most confusing and contradictory book that he had ever read. The Buddhist books were not without their quirks, but some of the philosophies were quite good. She even encouraged him to go to the local temple and learn how to meditate. Jack did this while being guided by a monk.

Sometimes he would sit there, and in the peace of the space, ask in his mind what his powers were all about. He was hoping for some sort of surreal experience in which someone or something would talk to him and tell him exactly why he had the powers that he did, but it simply never happened. One day, Jack was at the temple, and Nancy was playing with Michelle back at the house, only to have Michelle turn around and say, "Daddy" Before running off to have Jack pick her up. Nancy said to Jack,

"I thought you were at the temple meditating?"

"I am, I'm just bored shitless".

Nancy just shook her head and said to him, "What's the point of meditating if you're just gonna come home and play with your daughter?" He put Michelle down and disappeared. Thirty minutes later, he walked back into the house, saying that he was done with meditation.

What he didn't tell Nancy was that sometimes during meditation, his mind would drift, and he would have very vivid visions of holding cold, dead people who had died from heroin overdoses. It had got to the point that was why he had stopped. Nancy did note that Jack was feeling more settled, and he even said to Nancy one day that he could see that while in hindsight he could have done more for his mum, it just simply wasn't the way things were and that his father's death was an eye for an eye. One thing Jack knew for sure was that he was not a Buddhist Deity, and his powers remained a mystery to him, but the visions of cold, dead bodies from overdoses were troubling him.

Jack suggested that the three of them, with Kathy, catch a train down to Hua Hin, which was a beachside town where the king of Thailand had his summer palace. It was also a place where wealthy people in Bangkok went for holidays, and Jack got them two expensive villas, and Michelle would spend her time between Jack and Nancy's villa and Kathy's villa. Jack had been teaching Michelle how to swim at Bondi Beach, but it was a lot rougher. Here, the beach was a lot more child-friendly, and Michelle learned how to dive with her head under the water, including floating on her back. Jack was in awe that Michelle was getting to learn so much that was different to what he did working on the farm, but still diverse without the brutality and forced labour put upon him by his father. All in all, it was a great month, and Jack could see this was the future he wanted to have in his life all the time.

CHAPTER EIGHT

Jack caught up for a regular business lunch with Ronnie and Huang. Ronnie loved working in the United States as well as in Europe. He had bought himself an apartment in New York, a house in Los Angeles, another apartment in Amsterdam, as well as one in London. Jack had shown him how to manipulate his immigration files, as well as the stamps that were in his passport, so that there were no discrepancies should they be looked at by immigration officials or the police.

They were all now making a profit of hundreds of millions of dollars a year and were surprised that Jack was still talking about the cocaine trade. He said that it was simply an extension of what they were doing through the networks that they were using, and that it made sense that they'd be selling cocaine as well. He even said to them that within the next five years, they would be making billions out of it.

Huang was happy in Australia and didn't mind what Ronnie and Jack got up to outside of the country, as he still got a cut. But Huang could see that even he could make more money from cocaine in Australia if it was cheaper for their business and more available. Ronnie could see the sense in it, as his clients were also asking him for cocaine. Jack said

179

that South America was a very brutal part of the world, but he had come up with a plan that would eventually see them importing nearly 30 tonnes of cocaine a year into the United States, some of which could then be "shipped off" in their unique way to Europe and Australia.

Ronnie asked Jack if he wanted him to come with him. Jack replied that his first trip was going to be messy, and strangely, it would be better if it was just him by himself.

He informed them that the Drug Enforcement Administration (DEA) was starting to sniff around in the USA, and that local police were putting them under surveillance.

It wasn't an issue concerning the telephones being tapped, as they simply never used them to communicate with each other or other associates. Jack told them to command the powers to let them know if anyone was planting any wiretaps in their homes or offices, so that they could get rid of them or simply make them inoperable.

He also told them to make a command that they could not get photos of them. Huang said to Jack,

"How would that work?"

"They'll take photos of us with their cameras, but nothing's gonna come up when they go to process it"

He then added that the agents and police are going to know what they looked like, but they simply won't have a photo of them.

There was a drug cartel run by Pablo Escobar, but Jack could see that Escobar was determined to create his own trafficking of cocaine into the United States. This was because a lot of money was to be made in getting the drug into the USA, where it then got a big markup. Therefore, Jack decided to stay away from him and his cartel.

He put out the word to another drug baron and got a message through to him that he wished to buy half a tonne of pure cocaine with a generous offer of $US2000 a kilo to be bought directly from him in Colombia.

He had mastered the power of making machinery appear, and through Ronnie, had got himself a military pilot who had been given the powers, and they had bought an Iroquois helicopter. A meeting was made with the drug baron, and they appeared about 20 kilometres away with the helicopter in full flight, heading towards the drug baron's home. On board, they had $US1 million in cash that was in several bags. They landed not far from the house and were approached by armed men. They looked at the bags of money, and Jack said to them, "That's for Pacho".

Several of them took the bags of money and told him to follow them as they went towards what was a mansion in a rural area. He was taken into a lavish dining room where Pacho and his brother sat at one end with a bottle of whiskey in front of them, eating some steak and vegetables. He was not offered anything, and their mood was very blunt towards him. Jack explained to them that he wished to buy 500 kilos of cocaine with the view to buying a tonne of it at least fortnightly, which would be flown out by helicopter.

He knew that Pacho was having issues trafficking his cocaine into the United States at this time. Jack explained to him that he could help by selling some of the cocaine back to him in the US, albeit with a 40% markup, given the price that he was going to have to pay to get it into the United States. Pacho asked him how he planned to do that, and he said that at this time he was going to fly it out of Colombia, where he would then take care of it. Pacho placed a revolver on the table and said to Jack,

"Why shouldn't I just take the money that you've bought today, and leave you in a grave?"

"Well, I wouldn't have to sit here and watch you and your brother having lunch again"

Pacho pulled up the revolver and pointed it at Jack, but didn't pull the trigger, as he didn't want blood on his expensive carpet. The four guards in the room pointed their fully automatic rifles at him. Jack was told to stand up and to put his hands behind his back. They proceeded to use gaffer tape to tape them together. They then put a bag over his head with gaffer tape wrapped around his mouth and neck to keep the bag in place. He then got pushed over and had his feet and legs gaffer taped together. Pacho said to Jack, "Goodbye, I thank you and the DEA for your gift".

He was grabbed by two people who dragged him out of the room with their arms under his armpit and his head facing the floor, with the other two guards following.

They got so far down the corridor, and Jack quickly pulled his feet forward, stood up, ripped his hands and feet apart and knocked all four of the guards out with quick punches. He then ripped the gaffer tape off, as well as pulling off the hood from his head. He commanded that the men lying on the ground would remain unconscious until he was back on the helicopter and in the air.

He picked up one of the rifles, turned around and headed back to the dining room where Pacho and his brother were. He was going to kick the door open, but he decided to knock as Pacho and his brother wouldn't have heard anything that had happened in the corridor. Pacho said in Spanish, "Adelante" (Come in), and he went pale as Jack came through the room, pointing a fully automatic rifle at him. They were both sitting at the table, counting the money that he had brought.

His brother went to grab his gun, and Jack immediately fired a burst of bullets into his head. Pacho put his hands up to indicate to Jack that he was surrendering. He said to Pacho that he was in no way connected to the DEA and if he had bothered to do any research, he would have known who he was. He then added, "I know that you had a grave dug for me, I guess you will be able to use that for your brother". Jack turned the gun back to his dead brother and emptied the whole magazine into his brother's body. Thirty bullets were fired into Pacho's brother, which was a record for Jack that he didn't wish to repeat. As soon as the magazine was empty, he threw the gun at Pacho, hitting him in the chest. He then pulled his handgun straight out from the back of his trousers and pointed it at Pacho. Jack sat down at the long table, where Pacho was nearly three metres away from him at the other end.

Jack knew that he had a shotgun attached underneath the table, pointing at Jack's abdomen and said to Pacho, "Should you even reach for it, you'll be dead, so put both your hands on the table". Jack put his left hand out and made the bottle of whiskey in front of Pacho come flying across the table and into his hand. He then did the same thing with a glass and proceeded to fill it up with the whiskey and took a sip, stating, "Not bad". Now that he had Pacho's full attention, he told Pacho that he needed to make inquiries into who he was and quickly. Jack said, "I'll take my money and be back in two weeks, and you better have half a tonne of cocaine ready for me".

He returned in two weeks via helicopter and was greeted by the guards, who were far more friendly. He was again taken to the house and into the dining room, where Pacho got up from his chair and came around and shook Jack's hand and profoundly apologised, stating, "I should have made enquiries as to who you are. You had every right to shoot my brother".

There was a brutality in Colombia that Jack could never get his head around. His working relationship with Pacho was never as easy as it was with Khun Sa. He would sometimes have to beat him up or kill one of his associates just to keep him honest.

On Pacho's first attempt at giving him cocaine that was cut, Jack pulled out a baseball bat and smashed his right knee, leaving him on crutches for over a year. He found it infuriating and would have stopped it if it weren't for the money and giving Pacho the pleasure of a win.

Pacho offered him lunch, but Jack said, "Next time when we load up a tonne". The money was exchanged, and the helicopter was loaded with half a tonne of cocaine. He shook Pacho's hands and said that he would be back in two weeks for a whole tonne. Jack took off and proceeded to fly through valleys until they simply disappeared, and he reappeared at a warehouse in New York state with half a tonne of cocaine, where Ronnie was waiting for it. It was immediately distributed all around the world from there, including to "storage" in Ronnie's mind.

Jack even talked to Khun Sa about using a helicopter to get heroin out of Burma, as their needs were heading way beyond 200 kilos a month and would become a couple of tonnes a month. The four Vietnamese who worked for Jack were put on nice payments with the promise to keep quiet. Two of them couldn't help themselves and got involved with other traffickers, and ended up dead. Sam visited the two remaining ones and told them to stick to fishing, as their friends had stepped outside of Jack's protection.

With all of this in place, they were now the biggest drug traffickers in the world and by 1980, they would be billionaires. It was also when his nightmares and visions of cold, dead bodies got worse.

PART FOUR: THE RELUCTANT MESSIAH

CHAPTER ONE

The CIA was very active in the Golden Triangle and had become aware that Jack was seeing Khun Sa regularly, as well as probably taking heroin out of Burma. They had no hard evidence against him and nor how he might be trafficking the heroin, except they certainly felt he was buying it. The CIA and the DEA arranged a meeting with the superintendent of police in Bangkok with the view not only to put surveillance on Jack, but also to harass him. Jack had picked up on this as he'd seen people in the street in cars taking his photo, and he also became aware that there was going to be a meeting between a person from both the CIA and DEA with the superintendent, with a view to how they could put maximum pressure on Jack.

They were in a meeting room, sitting around a table with the chair near the door vacant and the door locked. The CIA agent had $US10,000 that he was going to offer the superintendent as an incentive to harass Jack. The superintendent said to them that there was a rumour going around that Jack was a Buddhist Deity and that he was hearing lots of things about supernatural behaviours.

The agents laughed at him. At that point, the door that they had locked opened, and in walked Jack with Lan. None of them were armed as they were in the Bangkok police headquarters and weren't expecting that they needed to be armed. They all looked at Jack in shock, not to mention at the 250-kilogram, two-metre-long tiger that had just walked into the room. Jack pulled out the vacant chair and sat down, and said to them, "If you're gonna have a meeting about me, you should have invited me".

They were all momentarily silent until the CIA agent got the courage to say to Jack, "I know that you're buying massive amounts of heroin in Burma". Jack looked at him and said, "I didn't know that was illegal given the amount that you guys are buying". Jack then rattled off a whole lot of information about CIA activity in Burma, Laos and Cambodia in the heroin trade, which took the CIA agent completely off guard. The DEA agent regained his composure and said to Jack, "It's the death penalty when you bring it through this country". Jack replied to him by saying, "Not even a gram of my stuff comes through this country. I just happen to live here". The DEA agent immediately said, "So you admit to buying it". Jack smiled and said, "I pay for a hit when I visit Burma".

The Superintendent was keeping quiet as he'd heard lots of rumours about Jack, and not only was he an opposing figure, but he'd walked through a locked door with a fully grown tiger. The Superintendent was Buddhist and was starting to think that the rumours were true. The CIA agent was unsettled given how much Jack knew about their activity in the Golden Triangle, and his mind was spinning as he knew that Jack was going to have to be terminated. Jack said to the CIA agent, "I know that you're thinking about killing me. Good luck with that".

The DEA agent continued to carry on about Jack bringing heroin through Thailand, with Jack saying to him, "What proof are you basing that on?" The DEA agent rattled off false information. Jack replied, "People will say anything to you for money". Jack was becoming quite annoyed with him, and next thing, Lan lunged across the table, knocking the DEA agent to the floor, mauling him to death. Both the CIA agent and the superintendent had jumped up with a fright. Jack pulled out his handgun and said, "Don't move anywhere". Lan had grabbed the DEA agent around the throat with his teeth, going into his carotid arteries, and the man bled to death in under 30 seconds. Jack then directed the CIA agent and the superintendent to sit back down.

Jack called Lan back to him, who didn't have a drop of blood on his coat. He tucked the gun back behind his trousers and said to them while pointing at the dead agent, "I want you to watch this". The dead body came off the ground and hung in the air with blood running all down the front of it. In Jack's mind, he saw the body being flung at the wall to his left with both speed and force, and as soon as the body hit that wall, he then flung it back across to the wall on the opposite side, hitting it hard before the body fell into a heap on the floor.

There was blood splattered all over the walls, and the CIA agent and the Superintendent were speechless. Jack said to the CIA agent, "That's what will happen to you and anyone else that follows should you come to kill me, harass me or my family". He then instructed the CIA agent to give the superintendent his money. The CIA agent pulled out of his bag the $US10,000, and gave it across the table to the superintendent.

Jack said to the superintendent, "That money is for you to leave me alone". He then said to them both, "That's the end of this meeting today, and I don't expect to be hearing from either of you anytime soon. Have a good day". With that, he got up with Lan by his side and walked out of the room. The CIA agent and the superintendent sat there for less than a minute, looking at each other while occasionally glancing over at the very bloodied dead body. The superintendent got up and left the room. He went through the headquarters asking people if they'd seen Jack and the tiger, but no one had. The superintendent gave very clear instructions to those below him that Jack was not to be touched or harassed in any way. He had just met an angry Buddhist Deity.

One day, Nancy came to Jack to tell him that one of the cooks had approached her about the fact that her husband was quite ill with cancer. He took a deep sigh and said, "Is she expecting me to help?" Nancy said to him, "You can but try". He agreed and went to see the cook's husband at their home. He was taken into a room where the husband was lying in bed, looking gaunt, with bottles of morphine around him that he sipped from. Jack sat down on the bed next to him and they spoke for a little while, but the husband was quite delirious. Jack asked for permission to put his hands on him, and he gently placed one hand on the man's chest. Jack simply imagined him being better, and for about 30 seconds, the man went from being quite gaunt to looking normal and very lucid.

The man grabbed Jack's hands, thanking him while the cook was hugging him, as they knew that he'd just been cured. Nancy said to him later that it was a good thing that he had done. Jack was far less enthusiastic, saying, "But where will it end?" Nancy didn't quite know what he meant, and he wasn't even sure himself.

A few days later, Nancy and Jack were returning from the park to the house, where a man was standing outside with a baby who were both clearly in distress. The man said to Jack in Thai, "Please help me". The baby was just in a nappy with no shirt, and Jack could see that it had measles. He asked the man if he could have the baby, and the man readily gave the baby to him. He soothed the baby by bouncing it up and down softly, while holding it to his chest with the baby's head just above his shoulder, and rubbing the baby's back with his hand.

He imagined the measles gone, and with that, the rash disappeared, and the baby fell asleep in Jack's arms with its head flopping onto his shoulder. The man was ecstatic, but Jack could see that he was also exhausted and thirsty as he had travelled quite some distance. He invited the man into the house, where they gave him water, iced tea and some food.

Jack was still holding the baby, who was sleeping. When the man had recovered, Jack gave him the baby as well as 1000 baht in 100 baht notes and told him to get a Tuk-tuk back home. The man then thanked him again and left.

That night, Jack was lying in bed while Nancy was asleep and rubbing his head, which was not something that he normally did. He was avoiding going to sleep as the nightmares of dead bodies were happening more often. It wasn't that he had a headache, but he did feel like his head was spinning. He knew that the rumours that he was a Buddhist Deity were growing and that the man of the child had heard them, as well as the cook and her husband were talking, and the rumours would just keep spreading.

Nancy woke up and turned round to Jack and asked him what was wrong. He said to her, "You know how I said the other night, 'But where will it end?' Well, I'm starting to think that it's not gonna end well".

Nancy said to him that what he was doing was very positive and stopping people from suffering, but Jack then repeated, "But where does it end?" He said that he was aware that there was a rumour going around that he was a Buddhist Deity. Nancy had heard about this as well, and she said, "Is that a bad thing?" He then said, "It won't be one man outside tomorrow, it'll be six sick people, then it will be a hundred, then it will be thousands". Nancy said to him that he'd been given a gift, so why shouldn't he give back? Jack said in frustration, "I'm not a Buddhist Deity, and I'm certainly not fuckin' Jesus Christ". Nancy then said, "Well, it's better than the thousands of people that you kill per year with that fuckin' shit you sell". With that, Jack disappeared along with Lan. Nancy didn't regret what she'd said to Jack, as it had been playing on her mind. She decided to let Jack be, assuming he'd be back the following day. The next day, Nancy was returning from her walk, and there were six people outside their place, all looking for Jack to heal them.

Over the coming days, the crowds got bigger, and Nancy was sending the staff out to explain to them that Jack wasn't there. When crowds started blocking the street, the police even got involved, moving people along at Nancy's request. Nancy was starting to see his point, but was also starting to worry as he still hadn't come home. After four days of not seeing Jack, she got in contact with Ronnie, who said that he had not heard anything from Jack.

Ronnie got back to Nancy within a short period to say it was literally like Jack had taken "the phone off the hook".

Nancy told him about the crowds, and Ronnie assured her that it just seemed that he needed some time out and would be back.

The days turned into a week, and Nancy was becoming very concerned, particularly given that Jack wasn't even having any contact with Ronnie. One night, she went to go to bed and there was a note on her pillow in Jack's handwriting which said,

"I'll be home very soon. I just needed some time to myself to think. I miss you all, love Jack"

Jack had taken Lan back to the jungle where they met, where he had set up a tarp and spent several days there. The war in Vietnam was over, and he knew that the area where he was would become a national park. They stayed there for several days, but his mind was swirling, and he was feeling confined by the thickness of the jungle and the visions of dead bodies. He'd read about islands in the South Pacific and decided to move Lan and himself to an uninhabited island that was near the Solomon Islands. He made them a very nice campsite just back from the beach, and Jack immediately started to feel better in that he could go for a swim. Even Lan loved jumping into the water. The beach that they were on had a nice surf that Jack could body surf in.

Part of Ronnie teaching Jack how to body surf was teaching him about rips as well as the golden rule, "Don't try body surfing in waves over two metres high". On this day, the swells were coming in at two metres, and Jack went out to catch a few.

He caught several, but he got dunked every time. Lan was swimming in the waves wash after they had crashed. Jack turned around, and there was a set of three that came in that would have been over two metres high. Lan was pulled into the crashing of the waves as Jack tried to dive underneath them. Then the waves got bigger, and Jack could see that they were over three metres high. Jack tried to run to dive underneath one of these swells, only to be put into a washing machine. He came up to see Lan struggling and could see another set coming in and swam towards Lan and wrapped his arms around him, telling Lan to simply stay still and not panic.

Lan went like a rag doll in Jack's arms as they came up, and Jack could see a large swell that had risen to probably over three metres high before it was about to crash on them. At this point, Jack had a realisation that they simply didn't need to be there, and with that, they were back on the beach. Lan gave himself a very big shake as Jack watched the huge waves come in. Jack knelt before Lan and hugged him while saying to him, "That was certainly unexpected. We will follow Uncle Ronnie's rules from now on". It never ceased to amaze Jack how something could happen that he simply didn't expect, and how he didn't always think to use the powers to get out of it. Lan seemed completely unfazed and still went out with Jack in more modest swells.

Jack sat on the beach watching the massive waves coming in before he allowed himself the luxury of oysters, shucked in Sydney, with beer and any other foods that he wanted as he tried to sort out his thoughts. His experience in the ocean, while having a level of trauma to it, taught him that even the ocean couldn't kill him. But he was starting to realise that the traumatic dreams were also going to stay with him forever until he did something to stop them.

CHAPTER TWO

Jack had Ronnie to thank for his discovery of alcohol, and for the nearly two weeks that he was on the island, he would sit and enjoy the sunset while having a drink. He was amazed that it made him feel relaxed and even think more clearly at times. He counted himself extremely lucky in that he could simply turn off the effects of it when he wanted to and never had a hangover. It had been a very difficult time with both his mum and dad, as well as knowing that the CIA and DEA were trying to mess with his life, albeit with understandable reasoning on their part.

Jack had now performed several healings, including bringing Nancy back to life, but he knew that he was not going to be able to save the world. He had spoken to Ronnie about this some time ago, and Ronnie had said that even though he had a lot of the powers that Jack had, he was not able to heal people.

He also knew that he could only do the healing by touching the person while being in their presence. In a world full of billions of people where hundreds of millions would be sick or dying at any one time, even being a full-time Messiah was not an option. Not to mention, he felt he was not being given any divine direction as to what he should be doing with these powers. If there was a God, he was feeling quite pissed off with it.

He had to admit that there was something very rewarding in healing people, but he could not see how he was going to do it openly without becoming some modern-day messiah. Given that he wasn't sleeping because of the nightmares, he decided that he might try another way of healing people while they slept, assuming this might be why the powers were torturing him with his nightmares.

He knew that the CIA were going to make an attempt on his life, but he'd be fully aware of how and when, so that was not of any concern to him. He had been thinking about what Nancy had said to him regarding heroin way before she'd even said anything to him, but he never mentioned anything to her. So it was of no surprise that she said it, it was just in the context and her timing that overwhelmed him. He felt stuck in that the drug trade had become his life, but the nightmares with dead bodies were getting worse, and he knew there was only going to be one solution to that. He needed to get out of the business. He knew how, but couldn't bring himself to do it.

While he was feeling guilty that he'd left both Nancy and Michelle for some time, he was feeling like he couldn't think straight. Being on the isolated island vindicated that decision to get away and spend some time by himself. He'd even conclude that he probably needed to do it more often.

A few days before returning to Bangkok, Jack got in contact with Ronnie and invited him to oysters and beer on the beach. Ronnie appeared that evening for the sunset, and Jack informed him that he would be heading back to Bangkok within the next few days and had left a note for Nancy, but that he had decided they needed to get out of Thailand for now. Ronnie had a major renovation done on the home in Sydney and informed Jack that he'd moved Nancy and Jack's room to his, which was far larger and had a better view of the harbour from the bed. Jack said that it was very generous of him. Ronnie replied that he was hardly ever there.

The bulk of the time that he spent there was on the balcony talking to Jack. Ronnie then added, "So long as I can sleep on the couch from time to time". Jack laughed at him and said, "I think with six bedrooms there should be one available for you". He mentioned to Ronnie about the incident at the Bangkok police station, and Ronnie said to him that it was time for him to get bodyguards. He didn't quite know why Ronnie was saying this until Ronnie said, "It's about the optics. People will take you far more seriously and leave you alone if you're surrounded by several massive and very capable bodyguards". Jack remembered the incident at the hospital and knew that it would have been more complicated if Ronnie and his bodyguards had not been there. Ronnie said that he would take care of it and organise a security detail for Jack.

Jack tried to talk to Ronnie about how he was feeling about the drug trade, but Ronnie was very upbeat in his maverick way and told Jack to "Stop being silly". Jack couldn't bring himself to tell Ronnie about the nightmares, and realised that it was also partly his strong friendship with Ronnie that was also making him avoid pulling the pin on their business.

Jack told Nancy to expect him after dark when the staff had either gone to bed or left the property. Nancy told Michelle that Daddy was coming home, and he appeared in the bedroom with a bunch of flowers. Michelle immediately ran at him with Jack picking her up and her wrapping herself around him.

Nancy walked over with tears in her eyes and hugged him while saying, "I'm so glad you've come home". She asked him what the flowers were for. He said, "I have never bought you flowers before, so I thought now was a good time to start". They lay down on the bed with Jack in the middle and Nancy on the outside holding him. Michelle lay face down on his chest before falling asleep with a cute, gentle snore.

Lan was walking around the bed, and Jack knew that he wanted to hop up. Jack asked Nancy if it was okay and assured her that the bed wasn't going to collapse. Jack commanded the bed to hold its structural integrity. If he hadn't, then the bed would have collapsed when Lan jumped up. And there they were with Nancy on one side, Lan on the other and Jack in the middle with Michelle asleep, lying on her tummy on top of him.

Eventually, Nancy said to him that she was so sorry. Jack said, "Don't be sorry", and assured her that she'd said what she had needed to say, and it was something that he needed a hear. He couldn't bring himself to tell her about the visions and nightmares he was having. He kidded himself about not wanting to alarm her, but the fact was that telling her would make the nightmares a reality, that he was still trying to deny.

Nancy acknowledged that he had a lot on his plate, adding about all the people who had turned up wanting Jack to heal them. She knew he would be aware of this, but just wanted to articulate to him that she saw what he meant. Jack then said that he was not going to be able to stay in Thailand for now, and asked Nancy how she felt about moving back to Sydney for a while. Jack didn't tell her what had happened at the Bangkok police station as he knew the CIA would follow him to Sydney, and he didn't want to worry her.

Nancy asked him about what he planned to do moving into the future, knowing that Jack was also having doubts about the trade that he was involved in. Jack said to Nancy that it was best that they just get back to Sydney, and he could tell her a lot more about it then.

Jack even repeated to her, "I simply don't wanna overwhelm you. Look what it does to me!" Nancy laughed. Nancy asked him about the place here in Bangkok. He said he would keep it for them all, as in time things would settle down and that they would be able to return here for holidays without him being seen as a Buddhist Deity.

Nancy did ask him why it was that he did not want to heal people. He then went on to explain that even though he'd given powers to Nancy, he knew she couldn't heal people. He said that neither could Ronnie, which meant only he could, as well as one other person that he knew of. Nancy asked him who that was, and he said, "The person asleep on my chest".

Nancy hadn't thought about Michelle and was understanding that it would be a big thing to ask of her. Jack went on to explain how he knew that he could only heal people by touching them and went through the numbers, saying that even if he was doing it twenty-four-seven, three hundred and sixty-five days a year, he'd be lucky to heal one hundred thousand people a year. He simply didn't believe that this was his mission in life, though he said he had given it some thought and had come up with an idea, as she was correct in saying that he had been given a gift and he should give back.

He told her about the last several nights, when he had taken his body to hospitals and located people with premature terminal illnesses. If the person wasn't asleep, he made them go asleep before touching them. He added that he had made it so that they weren't healed immediately, but that it was to happen over several weeks, though he had made their pain go away. He said for now that he wanted to keep healing people like this, in that it was a discreet way for the time being.

He explained that he would keep doing it and see what was happening to the people that he'd put his hands on over the last few nights. If it worked, he would keep doing it for now and try and work out how to maximise what he was doing. He said, "For all the powers that I have given to other people to grow my business, I'm still dumbfounded that this is not a power I can give to other people to do".

Nancy was relieved to hear what he was doing and could understand why he had run away from the thousands of people who turned up looking for him to heal them.

Jack asked Nancy if she was feeling ready to take her real body from one place to another. She said that she still felt reluctant, but he said,

"What if I hold your hand?"

"What are you planning?"

"I'll come back tomorrow night, I'll hold your and Michelle's hands, and we'll appear at Ronnie's house in Sydney with all our gear". Nancy said to Jack, "What about Kathy?" He replied, "I think she quite likes going first-class on the plane".

He appeared the following night, and Kathy was also in the room, whom he gave a big hug. Jack had taken Lan with him the night before and left him back at the house in Sydney. Jack handed Kathy a first-class ticket back to Sydney from Bangkok, and told her to expect to be well and truly searched at Sydney Airport. When Kathy asked him why, he simply said, "It is not because of any association with me, but because there's a lot of trafficking of heroin coming out of Bangkok through Sydney Airport, so you're going to automatically be a suspect", before adding that she would be fine and to just go with the flow.

Jack could tell of Nancy's nervousness while Michelle was quite excited. He said to Nancy, "This will be quicker than saying the word goodbye". Nancy said to Jack, "Do we need to sit down?" He laughed and said, "No, we can do it standing up". He then said to Nancy, "Which room would you like us to stand in in Sydney?" She wasn't sure as they started holding hands, and in the blink of an eye, she was standing in Ronnie's old bedroom. She had a stunned look on her face and then thumped Jack in the arm with anger, saying, "You didn't even warn me that we were going". Jack smiled and said, "I didn't want you to hesitate. But congratulations, you can now take your body anywhere in the world".

Michelle settled into their bed, and they went out onto the balcony where the butler had made them a platter and had some fine wine ready for them. Ronnie had let the staff know that Jack was returning, and the butler gave Jack an envelope. He took a sip of wine and then opened the envelope.

Inside was the deed to Ronnie's house that was now in Jack and Nancy's name, along with a note saying, "This is your welcome home gift". Jack told Nancy, who let out an excited scream. While Ronnie had kept this secret well, Jack was not surprised, given that Ronnie now had quite an impressive global property portfolio. For all of Jack's wealth, he owned one house in Bangkok. As they drank a bit more wine and enjoyed the food, Nancy said to Jack that it felt quite good to be back in Australia.

Kathy arrived back in a few days and had great tales to tell Jack about how customs had gone through everything in her bags, as well as having to be strip-searched. Kathy was aware of what Jack did for a living. He said to her, "You have my business rivals to thank for that". Kathy said to Jack,

"You don't bring anything in through the airport?"

"Not with the amount of searching they do"

Nancy was glad that Kathy was back, as she was dying to make love to Jack, but Michelle was clinging to him and sleeping in their bed every night, so they never seemed to have a moment alone. Nancy gave Kathy a nudge, and Kathy took Michelle to the botanical gardens, where they got some ice cream, leaving Jack and Nancy alone for a few hours. When they left, she took Jack's hand and said to him, "Come with me", as they went into the bedroom. Jack told her, "Please be gentle with me, and try not to break the bed", and she threw him on it.

Kathy kept homeschooling Michelle while Jack had expressed to Nancy that he was concerned that Michelle needed to be socialising with more kids her age. Michelle was showing no interest in going to school, and Nancy simply said, "She gets to hang out with a lot of adults".

They allowed themselves several weeks to settle back in, as well as meeting up with friends. Jack found this quite difficult as he had many friends down near Randwick Barracks, but he knew that he couldn't go anywhere near there as he had disappeared off the face of the earth to them.

Nancy and Jack went to have dinner with Sam, who is now well established in Sydney with his partner Bian. Bian was incredibly thankful to Jack, as he knew that Jack had done quite a bit to get him out of North Vietnam and into Sydney. Sam and Bian were not the first gay couple that Nancy and Jack had met. The butler and chef at their house were a gay couple that Ronnie had hired years ago. Jack and Nancy were both very impressed with the lovely house that Sam and Bian had bought in Lavender Bay, which had a terrace that they sat out on for dinner with a view of the Sydney Harbour Bridge and the Sydney Opera House. Bian also had a degree in law and accounting and was working for the firm that Sam had set up, which was now global with Sam as CEO. They even had a lot of legitimate businesses that they looked after, many of which were owned by Jack, Huang and Ronnie. Jack had been very impressed with how Sam had set up the money laundering side of things, and Jack was beginning to see how he could get out of the drug trade and move into legitimate businesses.

Sam had some Vietnamese staff, including a cook, and they had a Vietnamese dinner. Jack and Sam reminisced about how they met over many dinners with the Viet Cong General while he was in Vietnam, then met up in Cambodia and about their travels across the country. Neither Nancy nor Bian had heard these stories, and they enjoyed the tales that Jack and Sam were telling with many questions. Jack even told them about when they were robbed, while telling a lie by saying, "That Lan scared them off", while omitting how it ended with him shooting the militia leader in the head. Sam fully understood why he did this and didn't say a word. Sam himself had not told Bian about a lot of the violence that went on in the drug trade to protect Bian from the worry.

It was to be one of many dinners at Sam and Bian's place, including business lunches and dinners. When they were having dessert, Jack said to Sam, "Did you get that gift for Nancy?" Sam handed Nancy an envelope, which she opened and in it was a statement of the ownership of ten thousand shares in McDonald's. She looked at Jack, bewildered, and Jack said, "Coca-Cola is not up for sale just yet, but I promise to buy it for you when it is. In the meantime, you can still have your Coca-Cola at McDonald's". She jumped up from the table and hugged him while Sam and Bian clapped. In time, these shares would be worth several hundred million dollars. When they got home, Nancy hugged him, kissed him on the cheek while saying, "You did a good thing for both Sam and Bian by getting them both to Australia". Jack simply said that it took forged documents and money, stating, "It was nothing". Nancy felt that Jack downplayed the good things that he did for people. Jack said that he was happy to see that Sam and Bian were together, as he had picked up that they could not have an open relationship in Vietnam. It would even have been dangerous for them with the new Communist government. Sydney had a vibrant, growing gay community that Sam loved, and he was eternally grateful to Jack that he had ended up there.

CHAPTER THREE

Jack explained to Nancy about them getting bodyguards. He assured her that there was no risk, and she understood the idea of the optics of it. She even found comfort in having one or two bodyguards with her when she went shopping or for a walk, and they were very good at either keeping back or being with her if she wanted a chat.

Ben was the head of their security and had learnt the powers well and had found new creative ways to use them.

As Jack had learnt with Sergeant Brown, you couldn't make a dead body disappear before your eyes, but Ben had taught him that you could take them with you and make them appear somewhere else, then get rid of them.

Ben was also into rockets and outer space and told Jack about the perfect way to get rid of a body. Jack was amazed at the technique and asked Ben,

"You don't dump them out in the ocean anymore?"

"That's old school"

One night, Jack and Nancy had made love, and Jack was lying there in the afterglow. Nancy held him tighter while saying to him, "Have you looked into my family?" Jack had done this when she had asked, but had decided that he would not say anything to her until she brought it up again. So, he wasn't prepared that she had asked him at this moment, even though he knew she would one day.

It was an afterglow killer, and Jack simply replied to Nancy that he had investigated it. She, of course, wanted to know all the details, and he said to her that both her mother and brother wished that her father would drop dead of a heart attack. Jack added that her father was quite emotionally abusive towards them, including hitting her mother on several occasions.

Nancy said to him, "So what can you do about it?" He replied that he'd been waiting for her to ask him and said that he could make her father disappear. He knew that Nancy wanted details and even wanted to know that her father was going to suffer. He said that it simply wasn't the way that he did things.

He said to Nancy that it was her call and that if she wanted her father gone, he would make it happen. Nancy asked him about when it was going to take place, and he said to her again that it was her call to make. She simply said, "Make it happen".

Jack was going to try the technique that Ben had taught him and asked him to come along in case Jack fucked it up. Nancy's father was out on the farm, which was a wheat property that he owned. One day, Ben and Jack turned up in a four-wheel drive.

They both got out, and Nancy's father was by himself with no one else around who could see them.

He approached them, wondering who they were. Jack was very jovial and put out his hand, stating that his name was Jack, and he was from the wheat authority. Nancy's father put out his hand to shake Jack's, and as their hands gripped, Jack said to him, "I'm actually Nancy's husband".

Nancy's father went to pull back, but Jack had his hand in a vice-like grip and quickly did a side sweep kick, knocking Nancy's father's legs out from under him, where he quickly fell to the ground on his back while Jack was still holding his hand. Jack placed his boot on top of Nancy's father's chest while telling him, "There is always a price to pay when you sexually abuse children, particularly your own innocent child".

Nancy's father had a horror look on his face as Jack continued to say, "You took away the innocence of her childhood, and that's nothing she'll ever get back. Now you get to meet your maker".

At that point, Jack took his boot off Nancy's father and released his hand, and Nancy's father went flying up into the air. He yelled, but that quickly became something that Jack couldn't hear. Ben had told him to make an invisible cone shaped like a rocket head around his body to protect the body from the wind acceleration pressure as it accelerated into the atmosphere. They were both looking up, and Nancy's father quickly disappeared, and Ben added that he'd never done this with a live body before.

Jack looked across at Ben and said, "What the fuck?" as Ben said the G forces had knocked him unconscious, adding that, "lack of oxygen will kill him soon, the only suffering he's felt is the fear from you and from flying off the ground". Jack looked up, and they heard what sounded like a crack of thunder some distance away. Ben said, "That's the cone above the body going through the sound barrier". Ben had said to Jack that one of the advantages of this was that they weren't working with rockets and could make the body accelerate far faster. Then Ben told Jack that they didn't need to think in detail as to what was happening, except that the body would start to follow a trajectory to the curve of the Earth while rising to an altitude of 120 kilometres above the Earth to a speed of 25000 km/h. Ben then said that for something to go into orbit, it would need to accelerate to 30,000 km/h, and by making it go slower, it meant that the Earth's gravity started to pull the body back to Earth.

Jack knew that this would make the body come back at an angle of about 5 degrees to the Earth's atmosphere, with the cone having disappeared. Due to the speed and angle, the body would be completely vaporised in a few seconds. Ben said with some delight, "It will be one of those shooting stars you see". That spoiled things for Jack, as he never looked at a shooting star again without wondering if it was a body.

That evening, Jack and Nancy were sitting outside, and he said to her, "It's been done". She looked across and asked Jack, "How?" but he said that was not something that he was ever going to be able to tell her, except that her father was aware of why it happened. Nancy asked Jack what she should do from there. He replied that she just needed to wait. He had told her that the police would see that she was a part of the family and make the link to him, but that she wasn't to worry about that, as Ben would take care of it. Nancy was starting to become annoyed about how she was being linked to what Jack did by simply being his wife. She kept those thoughts to herself, as in this case, she had asked him to kill someone.

Nancy's routine in the morning sometimes was to come out and have a coffee and read the morning paper, and on this day, there was a local copy from the area where her mum and dad lived. It was front-page news that her father was missing, and Jack came out on the balcony not long after. He told her to send a message to her mother to say that she was aware of what had happened, with a view to going home to see her mum and brother. Jack could tell that Nancy was very worried about this, and he said to her, "Take Michelle with you, and I can come if you want".

Nancy contacted her mother by phone, who was understandably distraught about her father, but very emotional hearing from her daughter for the first time in over a decade. Because of this, Nancy decided to have nightly conversations with her mother via phone so that they could re-establish a connection. Nancy had told her mother that she was married and that Nancy's mum was the grandmother to a 9-year-old granddaughter. Nancy's mother was keen to meet them all, as well as understandably being nervous.

The farm was located nearly a 500-kilometre drive from Sydney. Nancy said to her mother if she wouldn't mind if they came by helicopter. Nancy's mother was taken aback by this, but at the same time said, "Yes, land in the paddock where the horses are near the house, and I'll make sure that they're not there at the time".

Jack had an Iroquois helicopter based in Sydney. His main reason for having it there was that he discovered a love for flying helicopters, and this one was great fun. Jack had the helicopter based at a Sydney airport, and when they were going to Burma, they would simply fly about twenty kilometres out into the Pacific Ocean and disappear, reappearing above the jungles of Burma.

Nancy rang her mum and let them know approximately what time they'd be coming, and that she would hear the helicopter probably about five minutes before they arrived, and that her husband would be flying it.

Nancy had explained to Michelle about going to see Nancy's mother and to call her grandma. They drove out to the airport where the helicopter was waiting. Both Nancy and Michelle had yet to have a ride in it, as Jack had been getting himself familiar with it along with the pilot that he used.

This was to be Jack's first time flying it by himself with Nancy sitting in the left-hand seat, and Jack had set up what was called a "jump seat" in the middle just back between the two of them for Michelle. The flight was going to take just over two hours, and then off they went.

Nancy was in a state of fear as this thing just lifted off the ground at full power without a runway and was nothing like an aeroplane until they got up a bit and started flying level.

Michelle was very excited, and Jack knew that he would be taking her on many joy flights. Jack did his training in much smaller helicopters that were also far less powerful, and found flying this helicopter to be like driving a high-performance car that handled and manoeuvred well. As he was coming down, approaching the house, Nancy pointed out a field to him that was not far from the house, where he did a landing that he knew his trainer would be very proud of. Jack shut down the engines, and they waited for the blades to stop before getting out. Nancy's mum and brother had been waiting at a gate, probably about thirty metres away, and Nancy got out first, and her mum ran to her, where they embraced, both crying. Michelle was then introduced to Nancy's mother, followed by Jack, who stood patiently back.

Nancy's brother had come up, and Nancy hugged him. He then shook hands with Jack and Michelle. Nancy's mum commented on how well she was looking and couldn't believe how handsome her husband was, not to mention her beautiful grandchild. Nancy's mother had lots of questions that she kept to herself for now, but she could see that the helicopter they had come in was certainly not a cheap one.

Nancy's mom had made them a roast chicken lunch with heaps of gravy and mashed potatoes based on conversations that she'd had with Nancy. It was a happy lunch given the circumstances, and Jack could tell that Nancy's mum was just so happy to see Nancy again, as well as meeting her granddaughter. Both Nancy's mum and brother were fascinated by hearing about how they lived in Bangkok for several years and were now back in Sydney, and Jack kept things simple by saying that he was a businessman.

Jack and Nancy's brother Tom went with Michelle for a drive around the farm, and Michelle was allowed to ride in the back of the Ute of the four-wheel drive, having a great time after Tom had told her to stand up and hang on tight to the back of the tray. For Jack, there was an odd feeling, particularly when they got near the field where Jack had made Nancy's father disappear. Jack knew that he wouldn't be here driving around with Tom without having killed Tom's father.

Tom said that the farm was manageable and that he'd be able to hire people to help during certain times of the year. Tom commented on the fact that Jack seemed to know a bit about farms. Jack shared with him that he grew up on a farm before going to Sydney. Tom shared with Jack that he'd been wanting to expand the farm, but that his father wouldn't let him and that he would now go ahead and do that.

He said that it was going to be complicated, given that his father had disappeared, concerning how long it was going to take to transfer the farm into his name. Jack gave him a card with Sam's name on it and said to him, "This is my lawyer, get in contact with him and he will help you out with all of that free of charge". Tom was very grateful for this, as he was finding the legal side of things overwhelming and knew that he was going to have to hire a lawyer. It had been over four weeks since Tom's father had disappeared, but Jack had read Tom's mind and knew that he was quite happy that his father was gone. He was just trying to suppress it, but Jack could even see that he had spent time out in the fields with quite a big grin on his face, knowing that the farm was now his.

Nancy and her mother had spent the few hours that Jack and Michelle were away talking and walking around the outside of the house and in the immediate area. Nancy found the house traumatising, given what had happened to her there. Nancy took her mum over to show her the helicopter, though her mother started asking technical questions which Nancy did not have the answers to and said, "That's something you'll have to ask Jack about". Her mum asked her how she had met Jack, and she lied by saying that it was at a party. Jack and Nancy had talked about how they would go about what they would share and wouldn't share with Nancy's mum and brother.

Jack had even decided for the bodyguards not to be around when Nancy's mother was about for now. Nancy had suggested to her mum about her coming to Sydney during their phone calls, and now that Nancy and her mother were reunited, and she'd met her granddaughter, she was far keener to come to Sydney. Nancy even said to her that they often went to Bondi Beach, which was a place that Nancy's mum had been a few times, but would have loved to have gone to a lot more if it wasn't for her bastard of a husband. Nancy could tell that her mom was also very happy that her dad was gone, and Tom had assured her that everything would be fine on the farm.

When Jack, Tom and Michelle got back, it was time for them to go, and Nancy said to her mum, "You could come back with us now if you like". Nancy's mum was hesitant until Michelle grabbed her hand and said, "I'd love to show you the botanical gardens and the art gallery". Nancy said to her mother, "Just come for a few nights and then Jack will bring you back". Tom also encouraged her to go and said to his mum, "Just go and pack your bags for a few nights' stay". With that, they all got on the helicopter while Tom watched it take off from the paddock. Jack told Tom that he was going to go out and do a large circle and come back flying low at 100 feet above their house at nearly 200 kilometres per hour, which Tom was quite excited about. Tom spent that evening sitting out on the veranda drinking several beers, and at one point even toasted his father by saying, "Good riddance you fuckin' asshole".

Back in Sydney, they drove back to Jack and Nancy's house. The bodyguards had been given at least a week off. Nancy's mum knew straight away that Jack and Nancy were quite well off to own such a beautiful big home on Sydney Harbour with their own chef and butler. Nancy and Michelle would go on to spend the next week and a half with Nancy's mother in Sydney, showing her around. Nancy had been thinking about her mum for years and had bought a home at Bondi Beach and had it done up several years ago in the hope that her mum would at least come and stay there sometimes. Nancy was aware that she needed to take things slowly with her mum, but planted the idea that this was Nancy's mum's house to have should she want it.

Michelle handed Grandma a card that she'd made and had written in, which also had a cheque for $500,000 that Nancy had arranged. Nancy's mum was overwhelmed, and Nancy, Michelle and her mum all had a big hug and cried.

Jack flew Nancy's mum home after a ten-day stay, hugged her and said, "You're welcome in Sydney at any time". Nancy's mum did move to Bondi as she wanted to get away from the farm with its bad memories, and to be close to her daughter and grandchild.

Tom would also visit when he could, particularly when Jack offered to come up and get him with the helicopter.

CHAPTER FOUR

Jack knew with the death of the DEA agent in Bangkok, that the CIA was investigating him with much more rigour, as they felt the he knew two much about their activities in the golden triangle and saw him as a security threat that needed to be terminated. He simply knew too much, and they even wondered if he was a spy for an enemy country. They knew that he was back in Australia, and they had linked up with the Australian Secret Intelligence Organisation as well as local police. The police that Jack had on the take were also telling him about the CIA's interest in him.

Because they didn't have photos of Jack, the only thing that they had was a description of him given by the people who had seen Jack or met him. They even found that if they got sketch artists to draw him, these pictures would disappear no matter how hard they tried to protect them. Jack knew that they'd be creating a profile on him and that they'd likely discover he'd served in the army through interviews with people who had served with him. They even found an ex-SAS soldier who told them about the incident of Sergeant Brown gunning down Vietnamese people, and Jack's reaction to it.

The soldier told them that Sergeant Brown had let them know in a coded way that he was going to make Jack disappear, but they both ended up disappearing. They asked the SAS soldier if they'd gone looking for Sergeant Brown and Jack, and they had, but he said that the jungle where they potentially went into was so thick that they couldn't see more than one metre in front of themselves. One of the agents said it sounded like the perfect place for a body to disappear, and the SAS soldier agreed. They knew exactly who had died in that jungle, as it wasn't Jack.

It was coming into the late 1970s, and Jack was not involved much in the business except for his fortnightly visits to Khun Sa. Jack had given the job of dealing with the problem child, Pacho, to Ronnie, who happily took up the challenge. He was always available for advice and certainly at times would get his hands dirty, but overall, the only thing that the CIA had on Jack was his fortnightly visits to Khun Sa. But even that was shrouded in mystery, as there were no immigration files of him travelling into any country in Southeast Asia and back for the whole time that Jack was in Sydney. Not only that, but Jack and Khun Sa would regularly change where they would meet up, making surveillance difficult. Even Forensic accountants could find nothing in any of the audits that they did with Jack's businesses relating to tax evasion or money laundering. Jack paid his taxes in full, which they found quite unusual for a criminal. The police told the CIA that manufacturing evidence on Jack was a lethal endeavour, and no one was game to do it.

Jack was aware of what the file they had on him had in it, as he had read it. But he decided that, given nothing was incriminating in it, there was no point in making it disappear, as the determination of the CIA meant that they would have it all written up again within a short period. The CIA had only interviewed the agent in Bangkok who had seen how dangerous and lethal Jack could be. There was no one else because they were all dead, and they had to rely on rumours that wildly varied. A CIA agent in Australia caught up with a few others and, going through Jack's file, they decided that they would kidnap Michelle with the view to luring Jack somewhere, where they would take him with the view to interrogating him using torture, and then kill him.

Jack was aware of this plan and spoke to Ben. Michelle had a routine of going through the botanical gardens and on to Farm Cove for an ice-cream, where she would spend some time enjoying the place. Everyone took turns at doing this, depending on what they were up to, but everyone loved going with her.

The CIA hired a team from a local rival criminal gang to do the job of kidnapping Michelle. Jack knew that this gang, and by proxy the CIA, were going to have no regard for Michelle's well-being or life. He could see that they were going to kill her once they had him. He knew that they were using surveillance in the botanical gardens to try and find a pattern of Michelle going through there and who she was with. Jack informed Nancy and Kathy that this was being planned, and they were understandably quite upset.

He assured them that he had the situation completely under control and they just needed to trust him. Jack spoke to Nancy and Kathy about setting up a routine for the time and who would go with Michelle through the gardens. Nancy was angry that Jack wanted to let Michelle be bait, even saying to him, "Why can't you put an end to this now?" He explained to her, unconvincingly, that this was a way to make them stop, and Michelle would not get hurt.

To give Nancy and Kathy assurance, he told them to randomly ask for him to come, and Jack would arrive, sometimes popping out of the bush with himself and several of the bodyguards. They did this for a few weeks, and both Kathy and Nancy were satisfied that regardless of who was with Michelle, she was going to be protected. What they didn't know was that Jack was planning on sending Michelle through the botanical gardens by herself.

Jack waited until one day when Nancy and Kathy had gone shopping, leaving Michelle with him. He told her what was going to happen and that he would be there. She was quite excited to be going for the walk by herself, and as she entered the botanical gardens, the team that had been surveilling her while waiting for the right moment could not believe their luck that she was by herself. Michelle had been sticking to a particular trail through the botanical gardens for a week, and the kidnappers planned to have someone go out onto the track after she had gone by with a fake police officer's badge to stop anyone else who was going to come through.

They even got a fake permit that allowed them to have a van nearby in the gardens in which they would drug her and put her in the back. She was partway down when she was approached by two men who went to grab her. She did a high Kung Fu kick at one man, sending him flying metres back, where he hit his head on the ground and got knocked out. The second man grabbed her arm, where she quickly broke his hand, before punching him in the head, knocking him unconscious.

There were two other men nearby, too scared to approach her. They waited as Michelle walked away as her father had told her to, before they walked out to drag their unconscious colleagues off the path. At this point, Jack appeared and knocked both of them unconscious and then proceeded to snap the necks of all four of the men. He had already done this to the man pretending to be the police officer, and Jack went down the pathway, catching up with Michelle, where they went on to get an ice cream and went down to Farm Cove.

After a while, they could hear police sirens, and Jack said to Michelle that it was time for them to head home for today, while assuring her that she could have more time at the gardens tomorrow. Michelle was disappointed, but then he picked her up and put her on his shoulders, which was something that she loved, and Jack took a completely different way home.

That night, it was in the news about the five dead men in the botanical gardens, as well as their links to organised crime. Jack explained to Nancy what had happened while first stating, "Please don't be angry with me". He knew Nancy would be furious at him for letting Michelle walk through the gardens by herself given the danger. She was aware that Jack had been teaching Michelle Kung Fu, but she had no idea that Michelle was that capable, and he said, "Like father, like daughter".

Nancy said to Jack, "I'll be back shortly", and went off and returned with a newspaper, which she threw with anger on the table in front of Jack. It was opened on a page that had a story about Susan's death. She said to him, "I don't want our daughter to be like her father". He was silent as he looked at the article and started to rub his head, knowing that this day was going to come. She then said to him, "How do I know that you wouldn't do this to me if I left you?" He started to say that he would never do that to her, and knew straight away that he was sounding pathetic.

Nancy said, "Well, let's give it a try, shall we? I'm going to stay with my mum". He said to her, "Can we at least talk about this?" Nancy said, "You need to get your shit together and do something better with your life. I don't want this danger that you bring to our lives". He again asked if they could talk, but she said, "You left me because you needed time out in Bangkok, well, that's exactly what I need". She then went and packed some bags and left.

Jack was numb as he hadn't seen this coming, though he knew that Nancy was going to find out about Susan one day, and had not worked out how he'd approach the situation. That night, Jack was angry at himself for not stopping the whole episode before it happened. He took that anger out by shooting all the CIA agents involved in organising the kidnapping and did something that he'd never done before, based on the trick that Ben had taught him. He dumped all four of the CIA agents' dead bodies at the front door of the CIA headquarters in Langley while they were still bleeding.

There were many meetings at the CIA headquarters, as many of those higher up had not been aware of what was going to happen, as the call was made at a more local level. As they got more details, they could not believe that Jack had so much good intelligence on them, to the point that they were starting to believe that there was a spy within the agency. This was true in that Jack was spying on them with his mind, but there was no one working on the inside for him. There was even a debate to be had about whether he could be recruited, but many felt that he was rogue and could not be trusted. There were even those who argued that maybe it was best that they just leave him alone, given the dead bodies dumped at the CIA headquarters front door from Australia.

But the main consensus within the group was that he needed to be exterminated, and they would make another, more well-planned attempt on his life sometime soon.

The CIA director made the call, and a plan was made on how to distance people at every step along the way so that nothing would come back to them. The bomb that was going to be used was constructed in the United States and shipped into Australia via diplomatic bags to the US Embassy in Canberra. They knew Jack didn't have high security around his home, and that the bodyguards did not patrol the outside area.

The plan was to put a bomb under his car, which they knew Jack used quite a lot. There was no concern for collateral damage, even if that was Michelle. One night, a man came onto their property and placed the bomb under the car below the driver's seat, then connected it to the ignition switch. They were aware that Jack was inconsistent with how much he used the car, with no routine and would just sit back and wait.

Not long after the bomb had been planted, the CIA director left Langley headquarters, hopped into his chauffeured car with a bodyguard and headed home. As the CIA director opened his front door, there was a massive explosion, killing him and destroying part of the front of his house. Forensic investigation would later show that it was the same bomb that had been constructed in the United States for Jack. Word had got back to them that the person who planted the bomb was shot dead, as well as all CIA agents connected to it in Australia. The CIA went into full paranoia about Jack having spies in the organisation, and a directive was given that he was simply to be left alone until further notice.

Nancy had no intention of weaponising the custody of Michelle against Jack. This wasn't because she feared him, but because of how much Michelle loved her dad, and she didn't want her to be traumatised by the fact that Mummy and Daddy were not currently together. But she made it very clear to Jack that he was not to expose her to a situation like that again, and he readily agreed.

Jack spent lots of time with Michelle, as well as taking her for swims at Bondi Beach, followed by ice cream. She would come and stay with him some nights, but Nancy, not being about, was ripping at his heart. He was also coming to feel tortured by the vivid dreams and nightmares. It had even gotten to the point that even if he made the command not to sleep, the powers would make him, with him having to still endure the nightmares. No amount of healing dying people was stopping that from happening. He knew what he had to do, but was feeling very paralysed to do it, but he had become very aware of his excuses.

For now, he tried to remain focused on his business as the nightmares tortured him. Sam had Ronnie, Huang and Jack over for a regular business lunch one day. Sam told them that he was having a problem with a bank that they laundered money through in the Cayman Islands. He had said that this was the main bank that they used, but that it had a new owner who was now asking for 30% of their money that went through it. Previously, they had been paying 10%. Jack asked Sam, "Is there any reason why we can't set up a bank ourselves?" But he stated that it would be very difficult for them to get a licence, given that they were known to authorities all over the world.

Jack then asked Sam,

"Can we buy one that's already set up like this dickhead has?"

"Yes, but do it through a legitimate company that you're not directly connected to"

Jack then asked if they could change banks, but Sam explained that it would come with its own cost and trust issues. He then asked Sam if he knew how much this new manager had paid for the bank. ,

"$US500 million. He also has very rich backers who funded it"

"Get in contact with him and offer him $US1 billion".

Sam got back to Jack within several days, stating that the man and those financing him had done their research on Jack, which is why he put the fee up to 30%. Sam told Jack that the man had said that he could have the bank for $US3 billion. Jack smiled and said, "Well, we certainly have met a greedy little prick". He told Sam to set up a meeting with the owner of the bank, where he would sign all the paperwork agreeing to the price that the owner had set.

Sam told Jack when the meeting was set up, and Jack stated that he only wanted Sam to be with him without any other staff. They arrived at the bank in the Cayman Islands by a taxi that they picked up on a local road some distance away. They were led into a large conference room where six people were sitting opposite them with paperwork in front of them. Five of them were introduced as lawyers, but Jack knew that two of them were hired thugs who were armed, wearing suits and pretending to be lawyers. The bank manager did not expect Jack to be as big as he was, though he was surprised that Jack had only come with Sam for a multi-billion-dollar deal. He also noted that while Sam was wearing a very well-tailored suit, Jack was only wearing casual clothes with a shirt with no collar. He noted that Jack had no bodyguards with him as their research had told them he often did, which was why he got the two armed guards. Jack and Sam sat opposite them, and Jack sarcastically asked the bank manager whether he'd changed his mind about the sum of money that he was about to pay. The bank manager said to him that he could pay more if he wanted to, with some of the lawyers laughing. Jack said, "Can we look at the contract?"

Jack and Sam took about twenty minutes looking through all the paperwork, which was over a hundred pages of lawyer gobbledygook of technical terms. They were able to communicate with each other by their minds, seeing that there were many loopholes within the contract. The backers had used a lot of blind trusts to own the bank, and the contract would not give Jack complete ownership of the bank and its profits.

The others in the room had got up and started having snacks that had been prepared for the meeting and making themselves a coffee. Both Jack and Sam had politely refused when offered something, but accepted a glass of water each. When they had finished reading through the contract, Jack politely asked them all to sit down again.

He sat back and looked at the bank manager and said, "Why are you trying to fuck me over?" The bank manager was taken aback by this, as he knew Jack had not communicated to Sam the whole time that they'd been reading through the contract. The bank manager said to Jack,

"I don't like the way you're speaking to me"

"And I don't like the way you're fucking me"

"What exactly are you talking about?"

Jack told him about all the problems with the contract, and how he was trying to keep control over parts of the bank and the profits through dodgy trust funds held within the bank's structure. The bank manager said that this was part of a standard contract like this, and that Jack would own those trust funds.

Jack shook his head and replied, "What a load of bullshit. This was always about ripping me off you greedy cunt".

The bank owner was offended and was about to say something, until Jack raised his hand and said with anger, "Just shut the fuck up". Sam got his briefcase out and handed Jack a folder with a much smaller contract in it. He slid it across the table to the bank owner, and he and his lawyers looked at it with them whispering amongst themselves.

The bank manager laughed and said,

"I asked for $US3 billion, and you insult me by putting $US250 million in this contract"

"That's the penalty that you and your backers are going to have to pay for trying to rip me off"

The manager was taken aback, as they had gone to great lengths to hide the backers. Jack then moved forward and pulled out a handgun from behind his trousers and shot both the armed men in the head. There were gasps by the lawyers, and the banker looked horrified as Jack pointed the gun directly at him. He said, "You either sign that contract, or you die right now, and I get your widowed wife to sign it". The bank owner said to Jack, "Okay, I'll sign". After the bank owner had signed all the relevant pages, Jack then pointed the gun at the lawyer next to the bank owner and told her to push over the file that he had just signed, which Sam checked and put in his briefcase.

Jack told the lawyer that he knew what she had whispered to the bank owner, in that they could get out of the contract and for him to just sign it if pushed. Jack then pointed the gun back at the bank manager and said, "I need to send a strong message to your backers". He then shot the bank owner once in the chest, hitting his heart. The bank owner had blood coming out of his mouth and was making gurgling noises as blood was flooding into his left lung. Jack knew that it could take ten minutes for him to die this way. The three lawyers were all stunned and were waiting to hear police sirens, not knowing that none of the sounds had left the room. Jack then rattled off the home addresses of the lawyers and the names of their children, and other family members, before stating, "If you in any way try and fuck around with stopping this contract going through, you will all die like your boss here. Also, you need to be very clear to the backers that they will die if they try and stop this purchase. They need to accept their financial losses here for fucking me around". The bank owner was frothing red blood at the mouth, and Jack stood up and fired a bullet into his head. Jack left the bank and waited outside. Sam stood up and passed his card to the three lawyers, who were in shock. He then told them that they would find the police to be unhelpful regarding what happened, and that there was no record of them even being in the country. He then said, "It's in everyone's interest that this contract is finalised". Sam then left and joined Jack, with them getting into a cab.

As Jack had been standing outside the bank, he thought about how the corporate world would use lawyers as hitmen and other unscrupulous tactics. He noted that he found it easier and quicker to solve these issues with violence. He then thought about whether the bank manager had deserved to die for his greed, which was one of the first times he had questioned why he had killed someone. He had also let the bank manager suffer for several minutes, which was something he never did. He was realising just how fucked up he was at the time, with the nightmares staying with him during waking hours.

Not long after this, Sam approached Jack and was surprised at how exhausted he looked. Sam said to him that the bank deal was finalised for $US250 million after the backers had heard what had happened to the bank owner. Sam then said that there were tens of millions of dollars owed by the estate on their house, a yacht, cars and a beachfront home and that his widow was going to go bankrupt. Jack said, "No wonder he was trying to rip us off, he was living a champagne lifestyle on a beer budget".

He then said to Sam, "Did she only love him for his money?" Sam said, "Yes". Jack asked about the lawyers who had been present and whether any were working for Sam now, which he confirmed some were. Jack told Sam to assign the job to one of them and give the widow $60 million, which would leave her comfortable if she paid off all the debts and didn't rack up new ones.

It was in this moment that he had a realisation that he was losing his sense of direction. He missed Nancy and wanted his wife back, and no amount of money or power was going to make that happen.

When Michelle was staying with him, she would sleep in his bed, and she was getting scared when her father would wake up in a fright from his dreams. He knew that he was going to have to make changes for the sake of them all, or he was going to go insane.

CHAPTER FIVE

Jack lived quite a modest lifestyle, and he wasn't into buying fancy cars or watches. He also basically only wore scoop neck t-shirts, and if they did happen to go out, he would wear a long-sleeved one. He only ever wore cargo pants and had developed a love for good-quality Italian bushwalking boots. Nancy didn't mind going to fancy restaurants every now and then and had tried to get Jack to buy something dressier.

For Nancy, there was an embarrassing incident one night when they booked a table at an expensive restaurant, and the doorman refused Jack entry based on how he was dressed. Jack had bodyguards with him and said to Nancy, "Let's just let Ben sort it out". Ben approached the doorman and handed him $50, then asked to see the manager. When the manager came out, he also offered him $50 to let Jack in. The manager refused, saying, "Doesn't this guy own a suit?" Ben said to him, "You either take the money and let him in, or we take you out on the street and bash the shit out of you while he goes in". Out of fear, the manager let them in. After that incident, Nancy again asked Jack why he couldn't have a nice set of clothes to go out in. He simply said to her that he liked what he wore, and that at least he mixed up the colours, but Nancy hated that he did this.

He invited Nancy out for dinner one night and surprised her by greeting her wearing a nice tailored suit. He knew what he wore out had been a thorny issue in their relationship, and this was one way of showing her he was prepared to listen. Though he couldn't bring himself to wear a tie, as he hated them.

Nancy couldn't get over how handsome he looked in it and walked up to him, putting her hand on the part of the unbuttoned collared shirt where a tie would normally be. She said, "You still can't bring yourself to wear a tie? But I must say you look very handsome in that". Jack replied, "I put it on, but felt like I was being choked to death". He drove her to her favourite restaurant, and when the maître d' saw Jack, he nearly fell over. The maître d' took them to a table that had a view of the Sydney Harbour Bridge.

It was a restaurant where Jack had been refused entry before, and even though Jack was required to wear a tie, the maître d' was so happy he at least had a suit on. The restaurant was completely empty, and Jack explained to her that he had hired the place for the night for just the two of them.

The time had come for Nancy and Jack to talk about what he did for a living. They ordered their meal and had a nice bottle of wine delivered, and Jack admitted to Nancy that what she had said had been on his mind not long after Michelle had been born.

He then went on to tell her about the nightmares he had been having, including the vivid visions that happen that had started when he was meditating in Thailand, which was why he stopped. He added, "I think the powers are telling me very loud and clear that they're not happy with how I'm using them". Nancy said to him, "Why didn't you tell me this at the time? He said, "I hoped it would go away and was in denial".

Nancy was aware of what Jack was doing for a living, but never asked him for details as she didn't feel the need to know. Jack told her about how he bought 100% pure heroin and cocaine directly from Burma and Colombia and controlled the drugs through to distribution.

He then added that distribution was broken down into two bits, which were wholesale, where they would cut it and sell it to dealers, as well as operating at a street level. Jack explained to Nancy that in the wholesale market, they were operating at about 70% of the global trade and that at the street level, it was about 30%.

Nancy asked him why there was such a big difference. Jack explained, "It's when it gets to the street level that it gets pretty violent with more moving parts. We tend to pick where we can work and not butt heads too much with rival gangs".

He then said that they cut both the heroin and cocaine to 50% purity, being very mindful to use benign products to cut them with. He even went on to say that they'd bought a pharmaceutical company five years ago, where they had a bulk product made to be used in the cutting with the view that it had minimal harm when used intravenously.

Jack explained that this was done with the understanding of the buyer that it was not to be cut anymore, but the profit the buyer put on it was at their discretion. He then added that this was also the case when they sold it at a street level. Nancy asked him, "How do you know people aren't cutting it?" He said that they were fully aware if someone went to cut it. She was going to ask him, "How do you manage that?", but she knew that the answer would be, "With brute force".

Nancy knew that Ronnie had been a drug dealer at university. Jack had to admit that it was the money that lured him to it. He told her about how he found £20,000 in John's house, and that when they did the job on the two crime groups, they had got £700,000 out of that. Nancy had known that Jack had got money from John, but didn't know it was that much.

She also couldn't believe the amount of money that Jack and Ronnie had got from assassinating the heads of the two crime groups. Jack stated that he couldn't believe how much money there was to be made from it, and given his powers, he was able to make the business very workable, safe and easy for everyone involved.

Nancy asked him why he hadn't taken full control of the global trade. he replied by saying, "We need competition to divert policing resources. Plus, given we are making billions, I fooled myself by thinking that I didn't want to get greedy".

Nancy then asked him the question again about how he felt that people died using the product that he sold. He said that he had felt conflicted by it to the point that he had tried not to think about it, but the nightmares were not going away, forcing him to think about it.

He replied, "I've dug a very big hole with this. I have tried to convince myself that I couldn't stop doing it, as that would take out 70% of heroin and cocaine from the global market, which would cause chaos. But the powers are being clear, that's no excuse".

Nancy asked him if he could sell the business. He simply said, "It's the powers that make it work so well, and they're not for sale".

Nancy was still trying to get over the sheer amount of money involved in the drug trade. He then said to her something that she wasn't expecting, "I'd like to try the heroin".

She said to him, "Is that because you want to, or you just want to see what it's like?" He said that he just wanted to see what it was like, and that he would stop when he had seen enough. Nancy agreed, knowing that the heroin that Jack would take had a known purity as well as knowing what it was cut with.

Michelle's tenth birthday was a month away, and Nancy said to Jack that she would help him so long as he stopped using it by then. Nancy had been thinking about going up the coast with Kathy and Michelle for her birthday. As they talked about it further, Nancy said that she'd help Jack get started, but then she'd like Michelle and her to be away while he went through the process of using it. He said that sounded like a good idea, and he promised that he would be there for Michelle's birthday.

Kathy had taken Michelle and had headed up to a place on the Central New South Wales Coast where they were going to stay in a house that Huang had bought. Jack had got the paraphernalia needed, as well as several small bags of heroin that they sold at a street level. Nancy came over one day, and Jack had assured her that he had given a command to the powers that the heroin was not to take his life, but that he wanted to feel the full effects of it. Nancy made up a syringe of heroin, showing Jack how to do it and how much of the powder to use, given its 50% purity. Nancy said to Jack that at this dose to not take it more than twice a day. They were in their bedroom as Nancy had warned him that he was going to want to lie down straight away, so he sat on the side of the bed.

She put on the tourniquet and showed Jack how to find a vein, and he watched her inject him with the heroin. It was under ten seconds when it hit him with an almighty rush of euphoria, and he fell back onto the bed in absolute awe of the high. Jack enjoyed this for probably thirty minutes before he fell asleep, where the nightmares were horrendous with rotting dead bodies from overdoses everywhere.

He found that he couldn't even wake himself up, as he had given the command to the powers to feel the full effect of the heroin, and being knocked out into sleep was one of those effects. When he finally got up a few hours later, he and the bedding were covered in sweat. He was still feeling drowsy and could tell that his mind was still altered, but nowhere near the level of when the drug hit him. Nancy had left for the coast, but left him a note to say that he shouldn't have any more today, adding, "Good luck, I love you very much".

Jack didn't want to try it again the following day, but the powers were now in charge. He didn't quite get the rush that he got the day before, but still liked the effects before falling asleep to visit hell. Then in the evening, he had another dose and felt that the rush was getting less. He continued for several weeks only to find that he was starting to take it to feel normal, as his body had become addicted, and he would feel unwell if he didn't use it. He then stopped taking it altogether and allowed himself to feel the full effects of the withdrawal symptoms kick in. After about eight hours of this, he'd had enough and made it stop.

It was Michelle's birthday, and he arrived at the house while they were down on the beach. Kathy was sitting on the deck reading a book, and Jack went out and said hello to her. They had a chat for about fifteen minutes. He spent the time admiring the view and was quite impressed with Huang's pick of a house. It was only a short walk to the main street of the town as well as to the beach, which Jack was to discover was very good for body surfing. Jack went down onto the beach where he saw his beautiful wife in a bikini, but held his lustful thoughts at bay for fear of getting an erection in public.

Michelle was playing in the sand, and when she saw him, she yelled out and ran towards him. He picked her up and gave her a big hug. Nancy also got up and ran over to him and knew straight away that he was not using heroin. After having a family hug, Jack said to Michelle, "Do you want to have a swim in the big waves?" As she was getting bigger now, she would go out with her dad and do some body surfing.

That evening, they all had dinner for Michelle's birthday, which consisted of roast chicken, lots of gravy and mashed potatoes, which happened to be Michelle's favourite food at the time. Jack loved that Michelle seemed to like simple things in life, and both Nancy and Jack had made a point not to spoil her with their wealth, though he knew in time she was going to be exposed to it. Nancy brought out a birthday cake that she had baked with Michelle, with ten candles, which she blew out.

Jack was terrible at getting gifts and had planned to buy Michelle a new push bike, but Nancy had bought her one a few months back. So, he handed Michelle a very large envelope and said, "Happy 10th birthday". He could tell that she wasn't thinking it was a very exciting thing just to be given a big brown envelope.

However, she screamed with excitement when she opened it as it was full of $5 notes that added up to $50. There was also a lot of other paperwork in there that she didn't know what it meant, and she handed it to Nancy. Nancy started reading through it and then said softly, "Holy shit!". Kathy said to her, "What is it?"

Nancy stated that there was a trust fund that Jack had set up for Michelle with $200 million in it, with her to get a third of it when she turned eighteen, another third when she turned twenty-five, and the rest when she turned thirty. There was also a cheque for $US200 million to an aid agency in Southeast Asia that specialised in giving out vaccines and running health clinics, including giving the measles vaccine.

What blew Nancy away more was that there was a deed to set up a global charity for people with drug addiction with a cheque for $US500 million. Nancy just looked at him, wondering whether he was trying to buy his way out of the situation he had created.

That evening, Jack, Nancy and Kathy sat out on a large deck of the house where you could hear the waves crashing on the rocks just below the house. Jack had found that when he was on the island, he loved going to sleep or even just lying, listening to the sound of the ocean. Kathy was about fifteen years older than Jack and was approaching her 50th birthday. Jack knew that it was in Kathy's mind that Michelle was going to grow up and that she didn't quite know what she'd like to do with her life then. Jack had assured her that she was family and that he would take care of her. Kathy excused herself, saying that her book was calling.

As she got up, he said, "This is a card from Michelle, but read it at your leisure, as it's too dark out here to read it". Nancy wasn't aware of this card, and Jack said that he'd spoken to Michelle about a month ago and got her to write it. About ten minutes later, Kathy came running back out and gave both Jack and Nancy a massive hug with tears in her eyes. Nancy was asking her, "What's happened?" Kathy showed her a cheque that Nancy could just make out in the low light, which had a figure of $20 million on it. Jack then told Kathy that Michelle had been wanting to get her a gift for her fiftieth. He suggested a sum of money, and that Michelle herself had picked the sum. He didn't add that he coaxed her to that amount. He then said to her, "If you do decide to retire at some point, at least you'll be comfortable".

After Kathy had left again, Nancy said to Jack, "Well, you seem to be in a giving mood at the moment. Got nothing to do with the heroin?" Jack smiled and said that the child with measles had got him to look into how poor the uptake and access to vaccines in Southeast Asia were, and the fact that children were dying from preventable diseases. He stated that he planned to expand on vaccine and health aid donations. He then added that the $US500 million was about him giving back from what he had taken from people, and that he was sure there was going to be more of it being given to help people with addictions.

Nancy asked him, "So how did it go?" Jack talked about the massive rush of the first hit, which Nancy herself had watched as he fell back on the bed. This was certainly how she experienced her first hit of heroin. He went on to explain how the rush got less and less, and how he found himself using more of it to try and make himself feel a sort of high. He told her about how he had allowed himself to feel the withdrawal symptoms. She said to him,

"And how was that?"

"It was fuckin' awful"

He then said about the horrific nightmares that he had while using it, which were worse than normal, and said to her that he felt he'd been told by the powers that enough was enough.

He told her that he was going to get out completely. He said, "I'm not going to be able to do it overnight, as I need to make sure that many of the people working for me are taken care of and not unnecessarily hurt, but I will work on it as quickly as I can".

Jack knew that this was not going to bring Nancy back to him, and that was something he was going to have to continue to work on. Nancy said to him, "You know how we went out for dinner at that restaurant recently? Well, if you continue to wear that suit to restaurants, you can ask me out on dates more often". She got up and went over, and gave him a gentle kiss on his forehead and said, "I know it's gonna be hard for you to get out of your business, but I wish you all the best and know that you can do it".

She turned away and walked back to the house with tears in her eyes as Jack disappeared back to Sydney.

Jack caught up with Sam for a working lunch in his office, where they had sushi delivered from a local restaurant. Sam was not at all surprised that Jack wanted to pull the pin on the business based on comments that he'd made over the last few years.

Jack spoke to him about how he wanted people to be looked after, just as if any company was shutting down. They talked about it for a while, and Sam said that he would organise files on everyone who was involved, and they could go through them and work out what sort of redundancy payments people would get. Jack was very clear that he wanted them to be very thorough and to make sure no one missed out. Sam told him that it may take some time. Jack said, "That's fine, I just want it done properly, and as you can appreciate, this needs to be between me and you".

Sam asked about Huang and Ronnie. He replied,

"I know that Huang is looking to retire and has been planning for his son to take over. I will talk to them in due time, as I get the impression that his son would much rather be doing something else with his life"

"And Ronnie?"

Jack took a deep breath and sighed, saying, "I have been trying to talk to him about this for years, and he just doesn't want to hear it, so we're just going to get on and do it".

Jack returned to see Sam a month later, where he was taken to a board room where one whole wall had hundreds of boxes of files packed against it. Sam said, "There are a couple of thousand files that we're going to have to go through". Jack knew that he had given powers to people with permission for them to give them to others, but had no idea it was this many people. He thought, no wonder the powers were screaming at him. Many of these boxes also looked at the business structure that they would be dismantling.

Given that Jack wanted to go through every employee in a thorough and fair way, he knew this was going to be a very long project. Both Sam and he went through their diaries working out times so they could spend time going through it in this board room, and one by one, they went through every file that ended up being nearly a year's work.

People who would be in hardship would be given an appropriate redundancy payment based on their current wealth. Many people would not be receiving any money as they were already quite well off, but they would receive an assurance that they would be protected from any repercussions when the drugs stopped flowing.

All of them would receive the same warning that if they got back into the business, that protection would disappear. If they decided to discuss their past business with Jack with others, the consequences could result in death.

Sam's law firm was doing a lot of work for Jack in legitimate businesses and charities, and it was not a warning that Jack needed to give him. Sam did make the joke one day that there was a thing called "client privilege", where he wasn't allowed to talk to anyone anyhow, which gave them both a smile.

Jack was also clear to Sam that as they went through the business structure, he wanted no one "left with their pants around their ankles" with regards to them closing shop.

The moment that Jack started working on this, the nightmares stopped. But he knew that if he was to have any second thoughts, they would come right back. As they worked through the files, he slowly felt the weight being lifted off him, and very much looked forward to finalising the business.

CHAPTER SIX

It was New Year's Eve to bring in 1980, and Sam and Bian had a big party at their place. Their place was a great spot to watch the New Year's fireworks, and Jack found that it was always a big thing when one was starting a new decade. Michelle loved Sam and Bian's house in that it was full of antiques and art, and Bian loved to show her the different things and tell her the story behind them. Sam had told Jack to invite whomever he wanted, and both Huang and Ronnie were there. Sometimes Sam and Bian's friends would invite unknown people who would get drunk and unruly, and Sam loved having his bosses about with their bodyguards who took care of any problems.

If the person kicked up a big fuss and made a scene, then they'd be thrown headfirst out onto the street to await an ambulance instead of a taxi. The event was well catered for with finger foods, and Sam had assigned a particular butler to Jack, Ronnie and Huang, who all enjoyed having their drink of choice. For Ronnie, when he was in Australia, it was Crown Lager. Huang liked to enjoy fine-aged single malt whiskey on ice, while Jack had a gin and tonic with ice. Michelle stayed up for the fireworks, and as Jack had decided to stand behind the crowd, given his height, he put Michelle up on his shoulders, so she had a great view.

Huang was now in his 50s, and it was early in the new year that he had decided that it was time for him to retire. Huang had taught his eldest son, who is now in his late twenties on how to run the business. Ronnie was quite happy for him to take over, though Jack had already had a private meeting with Huang and his son. Huang had bought himself a vineyard up in the Hunter Valley that he loved being at during harvest time.

He was spending his time between the vineyard and the house on the central coast. Jack had bought a house near him, which was going to be demolished, with a more modern, bigger home placed there to take advantage of the views.

Sam and Bian offered their house for Huang's retirement party, and not only were Jack and Ronnie there, but a lot of people who had worked for them. There were nearly one hundred people, and it was a great night with a mix of Chinese, Vietnamese and Thai food. At one point, Jack and Ronnie went and took Huang aside, where there were just the three of them.

Both Jack and Ronnie thanked Huang very much for not only teaching them Kung Fu but also for getting them into the business. Huang said he could not even begin to thank Jack for making their business partnership both safe for him and his family, but so prosperous and workable. Jack gave a gift to Huang of six bottles of single malt whiskey that were each over one hundred years old. Huang's face lit up, and he said to Jack, "When you're up on the central coast, we will open one of these and share it".

Jack said that he looked forward to it and added with a joke that he would make sure they would catch up when there was no construction noise coming from his place. Ronnie had bought Huang a gold Rolex and said to him, "This seems to be what people get when they retire from work". Jack asked Sam and Bian to join them, and they all thanked them for allowing them to use their house for the party. Sam was aware this was more than a retirement party for Huang and Jack.

Jack had been communicating with Ronnie about how he was planning to get out of the drug trade. Ronnie invited everyone to come over to New York and stay with him at his Penthouse apartment, which had views overlooking Central Park. Michelle was very keen to go by aeroplane, so Jack went about organising all the paperwork with their visas and aeroplane tickets. He warned Michelle that it was going to be a very, very long trip. Nancy and Kathy came with them, and Michelle loved being on the plane up until about the six-hour point when she started to ask, "Are we there yet?" Jack said to her, "Don't say I didn't warn you, we've got lots of hours to go", and Michelle allowed herself to be patient while reading books and playing games. They were in first class, and she even got taken up to meet the pilots in the cockpit several times.

They stopped over in Los Angeles for several days and took Michelle to Disneyland, where they all had a great time. They then flew across to New York in Ronnie's private jet, where Ronnie had a chauffeur-driven car greet them and drive them to his apartment that overlooked Central Park with city views, including the World Trade Centres. They would end up spending a week in New York with Ronnie being their guide. Being there in the wintertime meant that they all got to see snow for the first time in their lives.

Kathy was made aware that Nancy, Jack and Ronnie were going to be having a business dinner, and Kathy took Michelle with some bodyguards to the movies one evening.

Ronnie had set up a table in a dining room with the city lights, and the lights of the house were dimmed so that they could see outside but still see what they were doing.

Jack had got the recipe for the pork dish that he had with Khun Sa and had made it himself with the help of Ronnie's chef. They all enjoyed having some champagne while several Asian dishes were put out in front of them, as well as the one that Jack had made. Nancy took a spoonful of the pork dish, put it in a bowl and took a mouthful before saying, "Whoa, that is bloody strong". Jack laughed at her and said, "You're supposed to have it with rice". She did this and said that it was quite nice, but unique in a diplomatic way, as it wasn't something she loved.

Jack explained that it was diced up pork belly that was marinated overnight in a cup of white vinegar, a cup of soy sauce, with a few tablespoons of peppercorns and over twelve whole cloves of garlic, then slow-cooked. Jack explained that it was a Philippine dish called Adobo that Khun Sa had come to enjoy. Nancy said, "No wonder you come home stinking of garlic when you've seen him". Jack then said to Nancy that when he first started to see Khun Sa, they used pack horses to walk in from the jungle to pick up the heroin. Then he started using a US military Helicopter that would appear fifteen minutes away from where he was to meet Khun Sa.

Jack went on to say that now that he had his pilot's licence, they would enter the jungle over an hour away and have fun following the valleys and the terrain, with the helicopter ride being better than the roller coaster rides at Disneyland. He then explained to Nancy that when they would land at different places at Khun Sa's direction, he would get off the helicopter and sometimes go to a tarp that had been set up and sit under it. There, while having this dish with green tea and chatting with Khun Sa, they would chat for nearly two hours about all sorts of topics while the helicopter was loaded.

He said, "I'm going to miss those visits". Ronnie said, unaware, "What do you mean? Do you want me to do that?" Jack looked at him and said, "I have been telling you for some time that I want out, and you've done all you can to convince me to stay. I have been shown that these powers are not meant to be used this way, so I must stop and take the powers away". Ronnie couldn't believe what he was hearing and said, "You just can't take away the powers, people will die". Jack said to him, "I will take care of those people, and if they stay away from the trade, no one's gonna kill them".

Ronnie was dumbfounded and was almost begging him not to do it. Jack said, "You are a very rich man, and I'm sure you can be doing other things with your life, but this is simply the way it's going to be". Ronnie was almost in tears, saying, "You can't do it", with Jack saying, "I am going to do it, and there will be no more discussion about it". Ronnie was quieter and said,

"Have you spoken to Huang and his son about this?"

"Yes, they're both happy, and I'm sorry you're not"

Ronnie said with anger,

"Why did you keep me out of the loop?"

"Because you have continued to not want to fucking hear what I had to say".

With that, Jack got up and left the room. Nancy sat with Ronnie for a short while, but he was too numb to speak. She eventually put her hand on his and said, "I'm sorry it ended this way. I hope in time you find another adventure". She got up and kissed him on the forehead and left the room.

Jack had kept this meeting with Ronnie until their last night in New York, as he knew he would want to leave the next day. It was that day he pulled the plug on his business and with it the powers, with all the redundancy packages in place.

Jack had kept the next part of the trip a secret, and at JFK Airport, they boarded a Concorde for London. He had done his research and sat with Michelle explaining how the plane was going to travel at twice the speed of sound. He said that while the trip would have taken seven hours by a normal plane, this was going to take three and a half hours, and that they would be flying more than 20,000 feet higher than a normal plane. Jack was amazed by the acceleration of the plane as it took off with full afterburners.

He loved being with Michelle, enjoying the whole experience. All the seats were business class, and they all enjoyed caviar and other delights while on the fastest passenger plane that has ever existed. Michelle again got to have the pleasure of going up to visit the pilots and the flight engineer in the cockpit.

They spent a week in London going to all the sites, including the changing of the guard, before heading off to the stopover in Singapore. Singapore was starting to take off with developments that Jack was heavily investing in, and as Jack spoke fluent Mandarin, they went to many places in Singapore that tourists didn't go to, enjoying the locals and the local cuisine before flying back to Sydney. When they landed, Jack said to Michelle that she'd just had the pleasure of flying all the way around the world. She said to her dad that she could see why he had warned her that there'd be a lot of long flights, but she loved the Concorde most of all.

Over the following months, there was chaos in the trafficking world, but Jack was quite surprised at how quickly other players in the game picked up the slack. There was so much less chaos than he expected, that there were several times that he cursed at himself for not having got out years ago. He had tried getting in contact with Ronnie on multiple occasions, but Ronnie refused to speak to him.

Ronnie was not adjusting at all and was very pissed off when he found out that there was no storage of cocaine and heroin in his mind. He used cocaine regularly, and he was also very resentful that he was now having to pay for it.

He stayed in the drug trade using the contacts that he had, with the drug-fuelled delusion that Jack would come to his rescue should he get into trouble. Given that he was refusing to speak to Jack, it spoke volumes about his state of mind at the time.

He started to use cocaine more heavily and would regularly have parties where he would hire high-end escorts, and they would have drug-fuelled orgies into the night. Both the DEA and the FBI had noticed there was something different about how Ronnie was conducting his business, and were hearing through the grapevine that Jack had completely got out of the trade.

They saw an opportunity, and the FBI were able to get a female undercover agent to play the role of an escort. The woman had been very well trained in communication tactics to get people to talk willingly, and much to the FBI's delight, Ronnie became infatuated with her.

For the first time, the FBI were able to get wiretaps into Ronnie's apartment that were working. Sometimes it would just be Ronnie and the undercover agent drinking and snorting cocaine as she slowly encouraged Ronnie to tell stories about his time with Jack. Ronnie was becoming blinded by his drug-altered state and his infatuation with the woman. At first, he didn't tell her anything that they didn't already know, but on this night, he started to give out details that they were not aware of.

The agent was stroking his hair when suddenly there were loud cracks as the window shattered, followed by several quick whizzing noises, and Ronnie was struck with one bullet to the forehead and one to the heart.

The agent threw herself to the ground and, because she had not heard any gunshots, assumed that somehow a silenced sniper gun had been used. She looked at Ronnie, who was dead. She crawled across the floor and managed to pull down a phone and ring her fellow agents. They told her to ring 911 and that they were already on their way.

Jack and Nancy's home on the Central Coast of New South Wales was complete, and they were back together, spending their time between it and Sydney.

On that day, Jack was at Huang's house, and they were sitting outside drinking one of the one-hundred-year-old bottles of whiskey that Jack had given him. They were looking out over the Pacific Ocean and looking forward to the sunset. Even though the sun set in the West and they were looking to the East, it could still put on quite a show of colours over the ocean and distant clouds.

Jack had just taken a sip of whiskey when tears started to roll down his cheeks. Huang asked him what was wrong, and he replied, "Ronnie has just been killed". Huang took a sip of his whiskey and while looking out at the ocean, said, "Was it another crime group, or did you order it?" Jack said, "No, I did it myself".

They sat in silence for a few minutes, continuing to sip on their whiskey. Huang was aware that this was a possible outcome, as he knew that Ronnie had got back into the trade and that he had spoken out of line about their business in the past. Huang broke the silence by saying, "The thing about Ronnie was he always lived life hard, which meant he was going to die young". He held his glass across to Jack while saying, "To Ronnie, may he rest in peace". They had a sombre toast, and Huang went off and got another bottle of whiskey for them, where they watched the sunset and continued to talk into the night.

When Jack returned to his place, Nancy greeted him with tears in her eyes and came up to embrace him, and Jack started to cry. She said to him, "I guess it's all over now?" He said, "I hope so". He had warned Nancy some time ago that this could be a likely outcome for Ronnie and others, and she knew that on the night with Ronnie in New York, this was probably how it was going to end for him.

Several weeks later, Sam asked for a meeting with Jack, and while enjoying sushi again, he said, "Ronnie doesn't have a Will". Jack had developed a habit of rubbing his forehead or chin in these situations, and said to Sam,

"So, what does that mean?"

"His family are circling like sharks and going to put millions towards getting his fortune"

"And if they don't win?"

"The government gets the lot"

Jack shook his head and said,

"There's no way that he would have wanted his family to have his money, let alone the government"

"I can make a legitimate Will appear with all the money to go into charitable foundations?"

"How much of his money is off the books?"

"Billions, but that can also be directed into the foundations"

Jack sighed, saying, "I only know that he would not have wanted his family to have a single cent of his money. So, let's give it all to charity". Sam said to him,

"But what if the family fight this?"

"His mother and father are pompous greedy cunts, but I will make sure they don't fight it".

Sam looked at him while Jack told him the story about threatening Ronnie's father to dangle him over a balcony after a Christmas lunch many years ago. He said to Sam, "Ronnie wished I had done it". Sam said, "Well, I'm sure that's what Ronnie would want. I'll organise the Will".

When Sam produced the Will, a meeting was requested by Ronnie's parents with their lawyers, which Jack and Sam attended. Sam came in with a suit, with Jack in a scoop neck t-shirt and cargo trousers. Ronnie's parents' lawyers questioned with suspicion about when the Will was created and why it had only just appeared now, as well as why Ronnie would have left it to charities and not his family. Jack looked at his parents and said, "You haven't talked to him for over a decade. Why ask this bullshit?" The lawyers were not to be deterred and said, "Who's the executor?" Jack replied, "That would be me".

The lawyers asked more questions about the estate, including the value. Jack sat back and spoke, "I'd say it's around $US4.5 billion". He let this sit in the air before looking at Ronnie's parents and saying, "You have put up about two million in Australian dollars to fight this Will and will be lucky to raise $10 million with debt. You must fight this in the US courts. I'll bury you with $US20 million towards lawyers and take it all the way to the United States Supreme Court if need be".

Ronnie's father and the lawyers wondered how he knew this, and his mother started to cry. Jack said to her, "There's a toilet just down there with a mirror, go cry in front of that". Ronnie's father wasn't sure what to do as Jack was hijacking the meeting. The lawyers were trying to be combative to save their pride. Then Jack leaned forward with his forearms on the table and his hands clasped, looking at Ronnie's father, and said, "You and I need to do that thing where you look at the view from your balcony upside down, while I dangle you over the side holding you with one hand". One of their lawyers protested, saying, "That's a direct threat". Jack quickly glared at the lawyer and said, "Shut your fucking piehole".

He then looked back at Ronnie's father, who had gone pale and knew this was not a light threat. Then Jack said to him, "When you tell me you have had enough, I'll drop you on your fucking head. This meeting is over". Jack and Sam got up and left.

The lawyers were in it for the money and wanted Ronnie's father to go to the police about Jack's threats with them as witnesses. Ronnie's father explained what he had learnt about what his son did for a living before pointing at where Jack had been sitting, saying, "That man will have us all killed if we continue", and Sam and Jack never heard another word from Ronnie's family again.

Jack had already moved a part of his wealth into legitimate companies and was on the board of many of them. This was not without its dramas as he found himself dealing with some greedy psychopaths with questionable decisions, with little regard for the consequences to workers, the community and customers. He had hoped he had got away from violence, but often this was the only way to stop these people from harming others. Thankfully, the powers had no complaints. With his offshore money, Sam funnelled it into charity foundations. He continued with his nightly visits to hospitals around the world, curing the sick and dying. He felt it was good that Ronnie's money was going to help others, though this was an unexpected outcome.

He still found it troubling that he didn't know the source of the powers, but he had certainly found out the hard way that they were to be used for good. He knew that he was going to live for a very long time. Given the nightmares had stopped, he'd even decided to give meditation another go to see if the powers would give him some vision of what was going on. For now, he would try and teach Michelle as best as he could about the powers, and certainly not to abuse them.

CHAPTER SEVEN

Not long after Ronnie's death, Jack decided to take the two weeks that he had a year to himself on the isolated island with Lan. Nancy and Michelle would come and visit him separately from time to time. With Michelle, it was when the swells were good and there was good body surfing. With Nancy, it was for them to have time to themselves, often for them to walk around naked and make love in nature, including in the ocean. Nancy loved that Jack shared the island with them and could see why he loved to be there by himself.

Jack would often build a big bonfire on the beach in the evening, but would transport eucalypt twigs, logs and leaves from Australia so that he wasn't taking anything from the island, while at the same time getting to enjoy the smell of eucalypt burning.

One day, Jack saw a yacht on the horizon that was heading their way. He was unable to determine the captain's intentions, except that they were heading towards him. The swells were up that day to about two metres, and Jack knew that anyone trying to come in by dinghy was in for a hell of a ride. The boat anchored a couple of hundred metres away, and he could see that there was a man who was loading up an inflatable dinghy who had a large dog with him, and that he indeed was going to come through the swells to the beach. Jack certainly didn't mind that he was going to have a visitor. He wasn't sure whether to make Lan disappear or simply have him with him. He then decided that he and Lan were on the island first, and that the visitors would just have to accept that, but he was very clear with Lan that he would take care of it if there was a problem.

The man and dog left the boat in the dinghy, which was quite a decent size at nearly three metres long with an aluminium bottom and a strong engine. Seeing the quality of the dinghy and motor, Jack thought that the person was going to have a reasonable chance to get in, so long as they knew what they were doing. The man on the boat proved to have very good sea skills, with the dog standing proud at the front of the boat. He came in behind a two-metre wave, waiting for it to break before he accelerated, riding just off the top of the broken wave and then accelerating off it when it was only a few feet high before speeding up and heading towards the beach.

Jack met the man at the beach and helped him pull the boat up. The dog was the first to greet him and ran to Jack and jumped up, licking him on the face. The man put out his hand, and as they shook hands, he said to Jack, "My name's Oleg, but you can call me Oli". Jack could not get over how beautiful the dog was, and Oleg said that his name was Felix and explained that he was a mountain dog breed from Switzerland. Jack half-joked, "He's a long way from home".

Oleg had an Australian accent and looked to be in his fifties. He was only a little bit shorter than Jack, but was almost as muscular as Jack was. Oleg's hair was white, and he had very blue eyes. He was completely bald with a white beard that was over a foot long that he'd had plaited with a few beads placed in it, which he must have got done on another island. Oleg was shirtless with a great tan and had leather wrist bracelets and a leather necklace with a token that Jack knew to be a good luck charm for Polynesians. To Jack, Oleg looked part hippie surfer and part Viking.

He said that last night, he was about 5 nautical miles out that way and saw a red light and had decided to head towards it, as part of him wondered whether it may have been someone in distress. Jack pointed to the bonfire that he had set up for tonight and that he'd lit the night before, which was what Oleg would have seen. Oleg had brought several bags with him as he planned to camp the night, knowing that he was not going to be able to get back out through the breaking waves.

He asked Jack if he was okay with him staying the night, as the swells would probably be lower the following day. Jack said to him that he had no problem at all and welcomed the company. He added that he also had company, and Lan walked out with Jack telling Oleg that he was very domesticated and wouldn't hurt him. Felix went running up to Lan, licking his face before running around him wanting to play. Oleg dropped to his knees and encouraged Lan to come to him, and as Lan approached, Oleg dropped his head, and they put their foreheads together while Oleg rubbed Lan's head behind the ears. Oleg said to Lan, "You certainly are a big boy".

Oleg went about setting himself up a campsite with Lan hanging out with him and enjoying very rigorous pats from Oleg. Jack was surprised that Oleg had no fear of Lan at all, and he even did some play fighting with Lan and Felix, where Jack could see that Oleg was a very strong person to be able to handle Lan's size and weight. Oleg went back to his dinghy, where he had a bag of live unshucked oysters that he'd left hanging in the water. It was getting near sunset, and given that Oleg had the oysters, Jack went to his camp and made a bottle of South Australian Barossa Valley Chardonnay appear from their wine cellar in Sydney, which was five years old and took it to where he and Oleg were going to sit and watch the sunset.

Oleg was very impressed that Jack had the wine with him, and Jack was very impressed with how quickly Oleg could shuck an oyster, particularly given that Jack had still not learnt how to do this. He could shuck an oyster quicker than Jack could eat them, and they had at least four dozen between them that he'd got from another island.

Jack was amazed that Lan was lying next to Oleg with his head on Oleg's lap. Felix was lying next to Jack, enjoying being gently patted. Oleg asked Jack what he did for a living, and Jack said that he was a businessman and was on the board of several companies. Jack rattled off some of the names, and Oleg said that he owned shares in several of those companies.

Oleg said he had become an investor many years ago and was now retired and just sailed around the Pacific Ocean. Jack could see that the yacht that Oleg had was manageable by one person, but it was also a very fine and expensive yacht.

After the sunset, Jack lit the bonfire and Oleg set up a cheese table, where he had put some camembert cheese and salami that he cut up with crackers. He then pulled out a bottle of Penfolds Grange Hermitage that was a 1968 vintage. The wine was twelve years old, and it was not lost on Jack that this was the year that Michelle was born. Oleg said to Jack that he loved this wine and had a whole cellar of it on his boat, of various vintages. After they'd finished the wine, Oleg pulled out a bottle of single malt whiskey and poured them a glass, and they continued to enjoy talking about their lives. Oleg shared about his journeys around the world.

One thing that was disturbing Jack was that he was not able to read Oleg's mind at all, and had never encountered this before. Jack was enjoying the whiskey and asked Oleg if he could see the bottle. Oleg handed it over to him, and Jack noted that it had been placed in a barrel in Scotland in 1943 during World War Two, the year he was born. Oleg was taking a sip of whiskey and looking at the bonfire when he said, "Jack, I'm your biological father".

EPILOGUE

Jack sat silent for about a minute while his mind ticked over before saying,

"Well, that certainly explains a lot"

"I was very sad to hear about your mother. She was a beautiful person"

"Well, the same can't be said about the asshole I thought was my father. So, how much more do you know about me?"

"I have tried to respect your privacy, but I have read your CIA and FBI files. I must say that I'm very impressed by the sheer number of people that you recruited using the powers".

"I'm assuming that you also have them?"

Oleg nodded his head while saying, "As does my whole family". Jack looked at him and said,

"Go on".

"Both my mother and father have it, as does my grandfather. So, it's only natural that you would have it, as does your daughter"

"How old are you?"

"Sixty"

Jack looked at him and said, "It sounds like we need another bottle of whiskey, as this is gonna be a long night"

Oleg pulled a bottle of cognac out of his bag that was over two hundred years old. As he was opening it, he said, "We need an old bottle of French brandy as the family history goes back a long way".

Jack said, "I will need another bottle of Scotch whisky from 1943, as you tell me about how you came to meet my mother, and why you have only just appeared in my life today".

To Be Continued with
"THE RELUCTANT VIKING"

Acknowledgement

Everyone at the Oscars seems to thank their mum and dad, but in this case, I have a legitimate reason to.

My mother, as a fanatical book reader, gave me lots of feedback after reading the book several times, all of which was useful. She even gave me the idea to turn this into a Trilogy.

I thank my father for giving me permission and inspiration to draw on parts of his experiences growing up on a pineapple farm in rural Southeast Queensland, Australia.

My Grandfather, although a hard man, was in no way violent, unlike the fictional character in this book.

Instead of fighting the Japanese, where he nearly ended up in Singapore before they invaded, he redeployed as a rear-gunner in RAAF bombers. Here, they bombed the German war machine in Western Europe, based out of the United Kingdom, something for which I am very proud of him for doing.

Also, to my sister-in-law Jodie (sister Outlaw). I thank her for reading the book and giving me precise feedback. This consisted of her saying a keyword, followed by a frown as she forgot why she had written them down. Yet every keyword led to a fix.

Her feedback was also responsible for a major rewrite of the last third of the book.

About the Author

Mark Warman is an Australian author who is a jack of all trades and master of none. He has worked in Banana plantations and crawled under houses fixing pipes. From a professional wedding singer, he moved to the heights as a Clinical Nurse Specialist in his last incarnation, where he worked in Forensic Mental Health. Here, he not only dealt with some very unsavoury characters but also got to read their files.

It was also here that he got to wondering about the dance of violence and injustice in the world.

He then wondered if a criminal with supernatural powers could both commit the perfect crime and correct injustices. With that, a book series was born.

The True Norsemen were born as humans in Scandinavia before the birth of Christ.

It may go back further than that, but they simply don't know.

Born human, they live in the world knowing that their powers are to protect life on the planet.

But being born human also means that they come into direct contact with humans who would destroy the planet for personal greed.

This makes them natural-born killers.